AND
BABY
WILL
FALL

AND BABY WILL FALL

MICHAEL Z. LEWIN

WILLIAM MORROW AND COMPANY, INC.

New York

Library of Congress Cataloging-in-Publication Data

Lewin, Michael Z.
And baby will fall / Michael Z. Lewin.
p. cm.
ISBN 0-688-06880-4   ØØ736726
I. Title.
PS3562.E929A8   1988
813′.54—dc19   88-1089
                                                        CIP

Printed in the United States of America

First Edition

1 2 3 4 5 6 7 8 9 10

BOOK DESIGN BY BERNARD SCHLEIFER

For Iris Elizabeth Zinn

ACKNOWLEDGMENTS

IN THE COURSE of preparing for and writing this book I was assisted by a lot of people in Indianapolis.

Foremost among these has been Lieutenant Sheryl Turk of the Indianapolis Police Department, whose continued enthusiasm and technical advice have been a major help.

Three Indianapolis social workers also helped me a lot: Donald K. Wells, executive director of the Indiana Chapter of the National Association of Social Workers; Janet M. Myers, director of Professional Services of The Children's Bureau of Indianapolis, Inc.; Lyvon Hoskins, center coordinator of The Family Support Center, Inc. Errors of fact and stress that remain in the text would have been far more numerous but for their generosity with time and information.

I would also like to thank Alice K. Schloss, whose many kinds of support were vital during two very different visits to Indianapolis during the preparation of the book.

1

"I am not coming home yet and you'll just have to accept it," Adele Buffington said.

"You *promised* you'd be here by seven," Lucy insisted. "Mother, you're twisting me all up!"

"I promised I would try and I *have* tried. But, honey, I am not finished, nor am I close to being finished. I am sorry, but this report will have a real effect on the future safety of an otherwise largely defenseless child, and it needs to be right."

"At the expense of your own child?"

Adele ran her free hand through her hair. It felt heavy, so she tried to fluff it out a little.

"Lucy, you are twenty-one years old."

"Am I the less your child? Am I the less full of confused needs and insecurities?"

You're full of something all right, Adele thought. But she said, "Honey, I did warn you I probably wouldn't make it."

"You *said* you'd find a way to get it done in time."

"I said I'd do my best. I've done my best."

"Great," Lucy said. "You've just spoiled all my plans, that's all."

Her control loosening for a moment, Adele said, "Children are supposed to grow out of sudden sulks by the time they're your age."

"Now that it suits you, I *am* a child again, am I?"

"The longer you keep me talking, the longer I'll be here."

"If you're not going to be here on time, it hardly matters."

"Well, that's up to you."

"Fritz is arriving at seven-thirty, specially to meet you, Mother. He's terribly busy. You know how much arranging it took to set this up."

"I know that instead of picking you up he's always had you come to the campus to meet him, which makes me wonder why."

"If you're *not* here, he'll just think it was a come-on. I won't be responsible for what happens."

"Yes you will."

Lucy paused. Then with all the undertone of depravity she could muster she said, "Yes. I will."

Adele turned her face away from the receiver and sighed. She caught her reflection in the window through the slats of her venetian blind. But though she tilted her head this way and that, she couldn't quite see herself clearly.

"Daddy called," Lucy said, filling her mother's hesitation. The tone was suddenly cool instead of impassioned.

"To talk to you or to talk to me?"

"Me."

"What did he have to say for himself?"

"Oh, it was just to wish me a happy Valentine's Day."

He was probably in a bar somewhere. Massacred.

"But it's not for two days yet."

"He said he wanted to be the first."

"How did he sound?"

"Fatherly."

Drunk for sure.

"Did he want to make any plans, or what?"

"He's sending me some money."

"That's nice. Did he say anything"—Jesus! Don't bring up his not calling her at Christmas!

Somewhere behind her, Adele heard a cracking sound. It seemed to be on agency premises. She listened for it again.

Lucy demanded, "Say anything about what?" Her instant truculence showed she knew exactly what her mother had been thinking.

"I just heard a sound."

"Congratulations."

Adele frowned. Held her eyes closed for a moment. Returned to her daughter. "I was just going to ask whether your beloved father said anything about where he was or when he was going to see you next."

Coyly, "He *did* ask about the exact dates when my classes finish for spring vacation."

"Why?"

Airily, "Oh, just that he and Dolly are thinking about going to this little place in South Carolina and did I want to think about going with them."

"Sounds like a whole lot of thinking going on."

"Don't pour cold water on it, Mother. It could be nice."

"Yes. All right. I suppose it could."

"*And* I can think about taking a friend."

"I see."

"Well, it would be nice for Fritz to meet *one* of my parents, even if it isn't the one I live with."

"Thank you for that little bit of understanding, Lucy."

"You're welcome, Mother. But it seems like I'm *always* having to 'understand' about something or other about your job."

"I'm not cut out to sit at home knitting sweaters."

"I feel pushed out and unimportant."

You're twenty-one! Adele shouted in her head. Quietly she said into the telephone, "I hope it works out for South Carolina, honey."

"Is there any reason why it shouldn't?"

"I just don't want you to be disappointed"—Damn! Too far to stop now. —"If . . . if something goes wrong."

"I think I can handle disappointment, if any such handling should be required," Lucy said primly. "After all, I'm coping with the disappointment of my mother letting me down tonight when I especially wanted her to meet my new boyfriend and show her off because she's such a classy person."

"Now look, young lady—"

Lucy interrupted. "Oh, by the way, *your boy*friend finally called."

"Oh, yes?"

"He's been 'terribly busy' but I think his glands must have caught up with him because I had the impression he's feeling all smootchy smootchy now. I told him to call back at seven-fifteen because you were *bound* to be home then because you promised me you would be."

"Lucy, I—"

"Sorry, Mother, I've got to go and get ready. I just don't know what I'm going to do. Poor Fritz is the one who can't handle disappointment. Something about never having learned about delayed gratification. We've been doing it all week in psychology, so I understand that's part of what makes him so vital and attractive to someone like me who is always having to put off my pleasures, you know? Fritz is such a big cuddly baby in some ways. But soooo mature in others. Bye!"

The sound of the phone being hung up echoed in Adele's ear.

Do they ever stop trying to wind you up?

Do they ever stop succeeding?

Adele studied the telephone for a moment after she

replaced the receiver in its cradle. Why do I handle the simple problems of my personal life so much less well than the complicated problems in my professional life?

She leaned back in her swivel chair and swung round to look into the darkness through the blinds. She considered fishing out her mirror to look at her hair, but instead she interlocked her fingers behind her neck and breathed heavily and felt her insides churning in exactly the way her daughter had intended.

She hadn't managed to ask Lucy to check that the washing machine repairman had come. Much less to go shopping. The list was on the refrigerator. Would she notice? Would she even think about the shopping?

Of course not. Not when she could think about the Fritz.

Adele thought about the late-night supermarket between the office and home. How late was its "late"?

She ought to get back to the report. Ought. One of the words that is so easy to find in the brain and so hard to find in the more important parts of the body.

The report. The case. A young man who had dipped his three-year-old son's fingers into boiling water two years ago. Who wanted to start living with his wife again without the son being taken away.

A young man who claimed to be reformed. "I am a restyled personality," he kept saying.

Restyled. What the hell was that supposed to mean?

Some people believed him. Would the judge?

Adele knew that if she got back to work, she would forget Lucy's petulant games.

Ought ought ought.

Come on, get into *something!*

So, Al had called. At last. Where are you when I need you? she asked him in her mind. And answered, with fairness but no satisfaction, You're always available if I'm desperate enough.

A nice man, her Al Samson. A comfortable man who worked hard to protect her from his own sadnesses.

She felt a wave of affection for this middle-age "boy" who had been her "friend" for so many years. They had shared some precious times. She could just do with a warm close "time" now.

Should she call him back?

Yes.

But not till she had wound down a little.

Get up, look out the window. Jog in place.

Hup hup hup.

Adele laughed at the slatted reflection of her three jogging steps.

Perceptive, Al, when he had a mind to be. She could hear herself whine to him about Lucy and hear him say, "When she throws a punch, slip it. It's far more tiring for her to punch air than to make contact. I know. The boxers I bet on demonstrate it all the time."

Fritz. Why did Lucy have to pick complicated ones who—

Somewhere behind her Adele heard a door open.

That was definitely inside the agency.

Suddenly alert to the world, she turned from the window. She stepped to her office doorway. She looked at the agency's front door.

No one.

She frowned, sure, *certain*, that she had heard something.

She waited, watched.

And slowly, on her left, a figure emerged from the shadows of the interview room.

A man. An *enormous* man.

She was so surprised that for a moment she couldn't think of anything to say, to ask.

"Well, well, well," the man said.

2

THE man stepped toward her. Despite his size, his movement was springy.

Involuntarily, Adele backed into her office.

She flung her door closed and grabbed for the telephone, but in a bare moment the door had nearly come off its hinges and the man was in the room with her. In front of her.

"No," he said.

Their eyes held. The man's face carried a strange smile. Adele put the telephone back in its cradle.

The man turned out the office light.

Adele dropped onto the edge of her desk.

The only remaining illumination was indirect, from the screen of the word processor she had been using to write her report on.

"Just what do you think you're doing in my office, young man?" She asked, at last.

The man's rough face showed no response to her words, the "smile" seemed fixed on his face. It was an expression that made her think that he was capable of doing terrible things.

My God! He *was* huge! At least six eight.

Suddenly the man produced a torrent of words. He said, "Now I thought that, for sure, all *social workers* went home right on the dot when the old clock on the wall struck five. No way—no way!—was I figuring on having me a *social worker* here for a reception committee."

"What do you want?"

"You are a *social worker*, aren't you?" the man asked, as if she had told him so but he'd had a lifetime's experience of people lying to him.

Adele just stared.

"Wouldn't want to accuse someone of something like *that* if it wasn't right."

Adele knew she should say something. Instead, her mouth opened in profound silence.

" 'Course you are," the man said. He stretched a huge fist out toward her.

She leaned back.

A stubby thick sausage finger protruded from the fist. It stopped on a breast.

Was this what he wanted? Adele inhaled sharply. The finger didn't retreat.

"That yours?" the man asked.

"What?" Adele looked down.

The finger flicked up and hurt her nose.

The man laughed short, hard, humorless laughs and shook his head. "*Social workers,*" he said. "So fucking *stupid, stupid, stupid!*" The joke became anger.

Adele sat upright on her desk and pushed at the man's chest. "Get off!" she said. "Who are you? What the hell do you want?"

The huge man's eyes locked onto hers. He slapped her face, so quickly she never saw the hand coming.

The slap hurt.

The man flicked at the point of the breast he'd already touched.

The flick hurt.

The man slapped her other cheek with his other hand.

That hurt.

"Be good, lady," the man said. "You want to live, then be good."

Adele rubbed herself.

"I don't like nobody to sass me back. And I specially don't like sass from no *social worker*," he said. "Stand up, *social worker*. Stand up and shut up."

Adele rose.

With one hand the man enveloped her chin. From the other hand the sausage finger waved before her eyes like a nightstick.

"Listen," he said.

Adele watched the waving finger.

"I said listen!"

She looked at his face. The funny smile.

"What I want . . . ," he said.

He waited.

She waited.

"What I want is a file."

Though it was hard to speak, Adele tried to say, "A what?"

"A file. Where do you keep them?"

"What . . . what kind of file?"

"A file on the goddamn people whose lives you screw up. What kind of file do you think I mean?"

"Oh."

"Are they on a computer, or what?" He relaxed the hold on her chin.

She said, "We have a computer."

"That one?" He nodded to the silent screen that blinked remorselessly on Adele's desk.

"But the complete case files are in cabinets."

"Complete case file. That's what I want."

"In the main office."

"Show me." He released her.

She led him into the office, past desks and to the wall abutting the interview room where the cabinets were.

The man pulled at the top drawer. It didn't open. He rattled the handle, furious.

"My key is in my purse," Adele said. She responded to the unspoken order to get it.

He stayed with her every step of the way back to her office.

She found her key. They returned to the cabinets and unlocked them.

"All right," he said. "Now, sit down."

She sat in the nearest chair.

"Over there." He pointed to a desk across the room.

Grateful for the distance, she went to the desk farthest away. Thirty feet. Not nearly far enough. She looked at the window to the street. What would happen if she jumped through it? Movie images came into her mind, blood and glass. Then she saw an image of a cat pouncing on fleeing prey.

She turned back to the room. The giant man had taken out a flashlight.

Slowly, carefully, he studied the drawers' labels. Finally he picked one. He pulled the drawer open. Methodically he leafed through the contents.

Adele watched without moving. Almost without breathing.

It seemed to take forever.

She thought, I should be doing something. Memorizing what he looks like. Or *doing* something. Yes!

As the man studied the contents of the drawers he had opened, she eased a hand to the telephone on the desk.

Then her other hand.

She lifted the receiver. Even though she covered the earpiece, the dial tone sounded like an alarm bell to her.

She put the phone back and breathed hard.

Be good, lady, You want to stay alive, be good.

She sat like that for a moment. Watching as the man looked for . . . whatever it was.

Suddenly he turned the flashlight on her.

She jumped with the suddenness of his movement.

"Copy machine," he said fiercely.

She pointed to a wall adjacent to the cabinets.

"Show—" he began. Then, "I see it." He turned back to the file folder he had been studying.

He went to the copier. With his flashlight he examined it. He found the switch and turned it on.

"Does it need to warm up?"

"What?"

"Does it—"

"Just a few seconds."

One by one he took pages from the folder and copied each sheet.

The copier's hum was a relief.

Adele took the phone again. She punched 911.

She heard the emergency service answer. She bent down and whispered, "Police. Help."

"Speak up, please. I cannot hear you."

Adele jerked up as she thought the man was about to turn to her. But he didn't. He was gathering his copied papers.

"Speak up, please."

There was no time. Thinking to leave the phone line open so they could trace it, Adele pulled at the desk's drawers. The top one was unlocked. She slid the instrument into it. She pushed the drawer closed and then stood up. She began to move away from the desk.

As she did so the man turned to her.

"What do you think you're doing?"

"Nothing."

"Sit the fuck down!"

She sat at a different desk.

He stared at her for several moments.

Her fear reached a peak.

But the man turned away. He put the file papers into their folder and he replaced the folder in the cabinet. Then he closed the drawer. With a handkerchief he carefully wiped all the hard surfaces he had been touching. He folded the copies he had made and put them in a pocket.

He turned to Adele and said, "All right. Come here, *social worker*."

She rose and took a few steps toward him. She stopped ten feet away.

He moved toward her until the sausage was waving in her face again. "I didn't hurt you, did I?" he said with force. "I could of hurt you or killed you or done anything I goddamn pleased with you. But I didn't, right? So just don't forget that."

The sausage drew away. "I'm going out the way I come. Don't do *nothing* until I'm out."

He looked at her without blinking for several seconds.

Adele stared back and thought she saw in his smile, his expression, a softer edge, a melancholy.

But the finger rose to point at her again. "Don't do nothing you're going to be sorry for. I'm like an elephant. I don't forget."

In a moment he was through the door of the interview room and gone.

3

"Now you're *sure* he didn't try to get in your pants or nothing like that?"

"I told you exactly what he said and exactly what he did," Adele said.

"Don't get huffy, lady. I'm only doing my job." The patrolman, whose name was Wartman, raised both his hands in a mollifying, exaggerated and patronizing way. "You girls may be a whole lot quicker to call rape nowadays, but you'd be surprised what some of these suckers do that you girls are still shy talking about. Almost anything is an offense, you know. If it ain't for the sex side it's for the assault. Guy looks at you wrong, we could probably get him for it, in the right circumstances, you know what I mean?" Wartman was lanky, in his twenties, entirely confident of himself and extravagant with toothy smiles.

"I know exactly what you mean."

"Hey, I can get one of our own girls to come out if you'd be more comfortable talking to another girl. We got a good one, Cahisha Turula, out on patrol now. A bit quiet, but she's a real sweetie."

"That won't be necessary."

21

"And I think we should get you examined by a doctor, right away."

"I am not going to be examined by a doctor. There is nothing to examine."

"Could be a big mistake," Wartman said. "Change your mind in a couple of days and any evidence is going to be a whole lot weaker."

"The man came into the office to copy a file."

The young patrolman shrugged and scratched his nose and sighed and gave up his hopes of up-rating the incident. He asked, "So what was in the frigging file?"

"I don't know which one he copied." Adele felt fatigue. She wanted to get home.

"Yeah, yeah," Wartman said, "but what kind of stuff is in one of these files you got, that's what I'm asking."

"This is a private social services agency. Most of our cases are referrals that come to us after Welfare's sixty-day limit has been reached. In a case record we show everything we've done and everything we were sent when it came to us."

"Now this social work you do . . ."

"Yes?"

"What exactly would that be? Welfare money and marriage counseling and nervous breakdowns and stuff like that?"

"About eighty percent of this agency's work is in child abuse situations."

"So all you handle is kids?"

"No."

"Come on, lady. I know you had an upsetting time, but you're contradicting yourself now."

"Children are abused by adults," Adele said. She spoke to him stiffly. "You can't work on a child's problems without looking at the whole system the child lives and operates in."

" 'Course," Wartman said.

"And twenty percent of our work is in more general areas. Disabled people, for instance. We have a number of older clients who came to us originally as disabled children."

Interest evaporated. The young man scratched behind an ear. "So, you the head honcha here, or what?"

"I am in charge of this agency branch. We have seven storefront offices in Indianapolis. There is an overall administrator, Willy Hendricks. He started the original branch."

"Uh huh. Hendricks Agency," Wartman said, nodding. "So this Hendricks guy, is he going to be able to come in and help us?"

"Mr. Hendricks concentrates these days on fund-raising and the financial side of things," Adele said. "If you want to make a donation, he can help you."

"So there's nobody that knows what was in the file this clown was interested in?"

"The folder he took came from the A TO H drawer."

"How do you know that?"

"I saw him take it out. And put it back. But when I went through the drawer I didn't see any file that was obviously out of place."

"You *looked?*"

"Yes."

"You *touched* places he touched? Before our crime lab guy got here? Come on, lady. You ought to know better."

"The intruder wiped down everything before he left."

"Even so—"

"Even so, I pulled the cabinet drawer open with the edge of a nail file."

Wartman frowned.

"In case the handle hadn't been wiped quite clean. If there is a latent print there, I didn't spoil it."

"Oh." Then, "Hey, where'd you learn about stuff like that?"

"You're the one who's being inconsistent now. First I'm stupid and now I'm smart."

"And real, real touchy. But I can understand that. I'm in tune. A girl been through something like you been through, she's got a right."

"I'm not sure which part of this evening has been the worst," Adele said.

"You still haven't told me where you learned that stuff."

"My boyfriend is a private detective."

"Yeah?"

"So after, instead of a smoke, we talk about latent prints and surveillance techniques and how to kill someone with a rolled-up newspaper."

It was a joke and meant to be at Wartman's expense, but he missed it completely. He was being impressed by something else.

"A private detective?" Wartman repeated. "No shit. A real one?"

"What can I do to take a touchy girl's mind off her troubles?" Al asked.

"You can pass me the rum bottle."

He passed the bottle and said, "Relying on alcohol for tension reduction is the first step to serious trouble."

"Take a hike, gumshoe."

Al offered his own glass. "Maybe I should sing for you," he said, "or dance."

Adele poured him some rum.

Al said, "I'm afraid I didn't bring my harp with me."

Despite herself, the years of knowing him, "Your what?"

"My harp."

She looked at him.

"I bought this picture of a harp a few weeks ago. I like to look at it. It takes *my* mind off things."

"You mind is different from other people's," she said.

"I take that as a compliment."

Adele looked at her watch.

"Look, toots, what do you feel like doing?" he asked.

"I ought to call Willy."

"Uh huh."

"But I just don't feel like it."

"Then don't do it."

"You've persuaded me."

"Good."

Adele said, "I don't want to go out, but I also don't want to be here if Lucy brings this Fritz home."

"Where have they gone?"

"I don't know."

"Does she have classes in the morning?"

"I don't think so, but she's been making a big thing out of my meeting this kid."

"So who is Fritz?"

"Some kind of graduate student."

"You don't know what kind?"

"He's been on the scene for ten days. I don't know what courses he's taking, but she talks, with the greatest reverence, about projects he's involved in that sound half like sociology and half like business."

"A sociological entrepreneur."

"I do know that one of them involves interviews. That's how Lucy met him."

"I can see the thesis question now: 'Are phony interview projects an efficient way to meet undergraduate females?' "

"Could be. I don't know."

"Where's he from?"

"Someplace in Minnesota, I think."

"Ten days," Al said. He sipped from his rum. He frowned. "I thought Lucy was seeing someone called Arthur."

"Arthur couldn't cut it."

"I thought that was his charm."

Adele shook her head slowly. "The Fritz phenomenon has all happened since I saw you last," she said.

"Has it been that long?"

"You haven't been around much, *toots*," she said.

"Sorry. I didn't realize."

"I'm pleased when you have work. You know that. And I've been having a busy time, too."

"You're always busy."

"So my daughter was telling me emphatically earlier this evening. But there are degrees."

Al thought for a moment. "You know Jerry Miller?"

"Your police lieutenant friend?"

"He made second on the captain's tests, so he has hopes."

"What about him?"

"Well, his daughter has started dating an older guy. We're talking twenty-one or twenty-two with a girl who is maybe seventeen."

"Makes more difference then," Adele said.

"The first time this guy came to the house, Jerry waited in to meet him."

"Yeah?"

"Nobody said much, but just so everybody would know where they stood, Jerry left his badge and his gun lying out on top of the television set."

Adele laughed. "His daughter must have just *loved* that."

"She laughs about it, now. Look," Al said, "do you want me to check into this Fritz a little?"

Adele wrinkled her nose. "No," she said. "That wouldn't be right."

"OK."

"It's not the kind of thing a mother ought even to think about doing."

"True. So, what's his last name?"

4

"TINA!"

Tina McLarnon jumped and turned toward the voice.
"Oh, God! Adele! You scared me to death."

"I certainly hope not."

"My heart's going a mile a minute."

"Guilty conscience."

Tina leaned back in her chair and grew a soppy smile,
reliving what her conscience had concern for. "Yeah," she
said.

"So what are you doing here so early?"

The smile dissolved. Tina said, "I'm behind on my case
records, and Willy is due next week. You know how he
likes to pick victims."

"Willy will be here today, for sure."

"Oh, God!"

"But I don't think you have to worry about your case
records," Adele said.

"Why? What's up?"

"We had a break-in last night."

"No!" Tina shook her head. "God!" Then, "But things
looked the way they always do when I came in."

"The intruder climbed through the interview room window." Adele nodded to the room's door. "Can you remember the last time we had that window open?"

"Kinda cold for fresh air."

"He didn't break the glass. The police said it looked like it was unlocked. I told them it's always locked."

"The police called you back in from home?"

"No. I was here, working."

Tina's eyes widened. "When a guy broke in?"

"Yeah."

Tina waited for some detail. None came. "So what did he want?"

"To copy a file."

"Is that all?"

"Basically. Yes."

"What did you do?"

Adele said, "I cheered him on, since there was no viable alternative."

"And . . . did . . . was . . . ?" Uncertain how to ask what she wanted to know.

"And he went back out through his window. He just shoved me around a little. Nothing worth a *frisson*."

"Adele, how horrible. You must be feeling awful."

"I wasn't too bright last night."

"Should you be here today?"

Adele smiled. "Who finishes Florian Hatcher's court report if I don't?"

"Still . . ."

"Tina, have you been in the A TO H files this morning?"

"Nope." Tina held up three folders. "Lawrence, Simmenthal, Rosen."

"Do me a favor, will you?"

"Sure."

"Have a word with Anna and Martin as they come in. Tell them what happened."

"All right."

"And ask them not to go into A TO H. I'm going to finish Florian now—it has to be delivered to the lawyers this morning—but then I'll want to go through the drawer to see if I can work out which file it was that this guy took out."

"OK."

"And tell Patrick not to put *any* calls through till I tell him. I'm out of the office."

"I'll do all that."

"Thanks, Tina. You're a treasure."

"I'll even make you a cup of coffee."

"That would be most welcome."

Adele finished writing the report a little after nine. When she had printed a copy, she left the office and drove it to the lawyer representing the agency on Florian Hatcher's behalf. Against the "restyled" father.

Normally she would have stayed with the lawyer to be flirted with for a few minutes, but this time Adele drove straight back.

When she walked in she found Willy Hendricks pacing the floor in the area of open desks. All three team social workers and Patrick, the receptionist, were watching him wait for her.

Hendricks was fifty years old with a powerful frame and black curly hair that was peppered with gray. He clothed the advantages nature had given him expensively and he presented a genuinely formidable figure.

He had begun the Hendricks Agency when, as a graduate social worker, he realized that most long-term child welfare workers in Indiana have little or no social work training. This meant that unskilled people were routinely making critical decisions in life-threatening and life-influencing situations.

It also meant that qualified social workers didn't reap

the material rewards that come to successful practitioners in other professions, and this did not suit Willy at all.

So he started the Hendricks Agency. From the beginning he employed only trained social workers, and from the beginning the skills Willy Hendricks exercised most vigorously were those relating to organization and finance. He was a pistol at it.

Utilizing a capacity for direct and personal contact with whoever he was speaking to—no matter what he said or how he said it—he led the agency to a rapid growth. This was despite legislatively inspired trends to focus social work development in Indiana on mental health centers. Respect for the quality of the agency's work was widespread.

Willy did all the hiring and firing, and he also did all the accounts himself.

Adele Buffington, as a disaffected probation officer, had joined Hendricks when the 34th Street branch, Hendricks's third, opened. She'd worked for him for six years now, in charge of the social work side of the running of the branch.

"Adele!" Willy said warmly, as she walked through the door. "Are you all right, babe? Did the bastard hurt you?"

"I'm OK," she said.

"I was shocked. Absolutely dumbfounded. I hope you really are in tacto, kid. I'll murder the bum, if they ever catch him."

"That's not a very enlightened attitude."

"I'm a Hoosier. Since when am I expected to be a member of the twentieth century?" He turned to the other social workers, Tina, Anna Pike and Martin Cretney. "This woman you work for is a special person, a really special person. I hope you appreciate that. I can't think of any other social worker in this city who has the combination of human sensitivity and social overview that this woman has. She's one in a million."

Astonishingly, Hendricks turned to Adele and began to applaud.

Astonishingly, the other people in the room joined in.

Adele watched the performance without having any idea how to respond.

Hendricks said, "But come on. Let's confab."

"OK."

"Your office. Unless you'd rather get out. God, but this place must seem a prison to you sometimes, sweetheart."

"My office is fine."

With broad smiles and sweeping arm gestures, Willy followed Adele into her office and pulled the door closed behind him.

Adele said, "You know damn well none of them are taken in by all the cheerleading."

"But, darling, they expect a show from me."

"And you love to give it." Adele smiled.

"They also expect to see me giving support when one of my people has trouble." He looked at her. "You look tired, babe."

"How else should I look?"

Adele sat.

Hendricks turned his back on her and studied a poster painting of a woman's face that was framed and hanging on the wall. The title was incorporated in the painting. It was called "Face."

"Nice," he said. "Who did it?"

"My daughter."

"Ah, the estimable Lucy."

"Yes."

There was silence.

Adele said, "You're getting position on something, Willy. I'm too tired to wait much longer for it."

"You should have called me," he said, turning to her. He was angry. "Why the hell didn't you call me?"

"I tried. The line was busy."

"You should have tried again."

"I did. It was busy again."

"Don't you know how important my keeping on top of something like this is? You *must* know."

"Willy, how about a little understanding on your part?"

"Tina said you weren't hurt."

"Great."

"Look, doll, you know how precarious our funding is, how *political* it is. Any excuse, and the benevolent city fathers and their business friends will chop the balls out of our grants and put their cash into yet another Olympic-size chamber pot so they can host the annual piss-in-the-wind world championships. I have *got* to know about anything that *happens*, right a-goddamn-way."

"The police informed you, didn't they?"

"And I felt like an idiot because my own staff member, my most valued employee—and that's not PR, you really are—because my own goddamn most valuable player hadn't had the common courtesy to call me first."

"So fire me."

"Come on, baby babe! That's not what I mean. I was just hurt, *hurt*! What do you think—I don't feel pain? Because I'm out there smiling and hustling and conning all the time, I don't have emotions? I shed tears, real tears, when I realized that I had heard about a break-in at one of my own offices from a complete stranger."

"Well, I am sorry, but after everything that—"

"And it's more than just the personal feelings I have, too, if you don't value those. I'll give you an example. I was talking to a man just yesterday who, if I had *known* about this, I am absolutely certain I could have got to stump up money for better security arrangements. He was all warm and willing, no problem."

"It didn't happen until last night, Willy."

"I'm trying to help you understand what my life is like, trying to keep this place going."

"I'm sure you scored for something."

"That's not the issue. The issue is that you should have

made more effort to inform me. A note through my door, Adele.. Anything!"

"To tell you the truth, Willy, I just didn't feel up to it. I had had a rough time here, and then the cops who arrived were as sensitive as sandpaper."

Hendricks stood looking at her for several seconds. Theatrically, he shrugged. "Water under the bridge," he said. "Hey, I'm not *criticizing* you. I hope you know that." But without leaving time for her to respond he went on to ask, "So, *are* you OK?"

"Yeah. I guess."

"All right," Willy said. "I won't go on. I've made my point."

"You've made your point."

"It's just I like to think I run a tight ship. You know it's the only way we keep from sinking. And I was a little disappointed, that's all." He opened the door. "I'd like to stick around, show the flag, but I can't. I'll be back to have a look through some of the records next week, if I get a chance. Make sure everything is shipshape. And I may stop by with a couple of state senators. All right?"

5

WILLY Hendricks smiled and nodded his way from Adele's office to the agency's front door. As he arrived at it, a severely stooped old woman, wrapped in black garments, entered.

He stepped back and held the door. The stooped old woman looked up sideways as she passed him, and said, in a remarkably strong and clear voice, "Thank you, young man."

" 'Young man'! What a charmer you are, my dear. It is always a pleasure to hold a door for a gracious lady. It truly is." Hendricks bowed as the woman continued into the room, then he swept out the door.

From her sideways perspective on the world, the old woman looked after him. So did everyone else in the office.

It was a perfect Willy exit.

Tina McLarnon rose and went to see to the woman in black.

"It's about my grandson, Clyde," the old woman said. "You can sort it out, I'm sure."

"I'll do my best," Tina said.

She led the woman to her desk and both sat down. Tina asked, "What is the problem?"

"He's twelve."

Tina nodded and opened a notebook.

"He's doing sexual intercourse in the garage with the girl next door."

Tina looked up.

"With one of the girls next door, for sure. But I wouldn't be surprised if it wasn't all three."

"But . . . But how do you know?"

"I saw them at it."

"You did?"

"They were all there, the three girls and Clyde, in the garage. Then Norma pulled at my Clyde and they did it to each other, and both Corinne and that Mary Lou cheered them on."

"Good heavens," Tina said.

The old woman shifted sideways in her chair to get a better look at Tina, rotating her face up so that Tina saw the bright brown eyes blazing with indignation. The woman said, "That little hussy Norma may only be nine years old, but she's leading my Clyde astray."

"Nine? This girl is nine?"

"I don't mind about *her*. She's probably been at it for years. It's Clyde I got concern about. He's a real good little boy, and down at the Cubs they say he's something like a genius, and I don't want some little slut of a neighbor girl ruining his chances for a good job."

They began on the matter of names and addresses.

The other social workers—Anna Pike and Martin Cretney—sat in Adele's office. The switchboard operator and receptionist, Patrick Cheese, stood in the doorway where he could see his switchboard.

Martin said, "Thanks for letting us have a few moments of your time, Adele."

"Of course."

Martin Cretney, a bachelor of forty and without apparent career ambitions, was the unofficial office spokesman when the field social workers wanted to raise administrative issues with higher management. He was the longest-serving of the field workers and had worked for Willy Hendricks longer than Adele.

Anna Pike, a small, dark, finely drawn and irritable woman in her mid-twenties, asked Adele, "So, are you all right, or what?"

"Yes, of course I'm all right."

"You can understand why we ask," Martin said. "We get to work and you're locked in your office, incommunicado. Then when your door finally does open, you run out without a word. And then the big chief arrives and stands around complaining about how busy he is, but he still waits till you get back so you and he can hole up for a while in here. Things are obviously going on. We heard there was a break-in from Tina, and she told us you don't want anybody to use the A TO H files, but we feel that we're entitled, surely, to be filled in."

"Of course you are," Adele said. "Things have just been happening so very fast."

"Oh, oh," Patrick said, and he left the doorway.

"There was an intruder last night," Adele said. "A man came in while I was working—"

"You were actually here?" Anna asked.

"Yes. The Florian Hatcher report had to be in this morning."

"Ah," Martin said. "Hence the isolation and the early-morning dash."

"That's right. I was interrupted last night and had to get it finished and delivered first thing."

"But you were here," Anna said, "when a man broke in?"

"Yes."

"That's absolutely disgusting," Anna said.

Patrick reappeared in the doorway. He said, "Excuse me, Adele. Are you taking calls?"

"Are you offering me one?"

Patrick nodded. Then his face turned pink. "It's a guy that called this morning, while you were out. A policeman. I didn't tell you. Sorry."

"I guess I'll take it," Adele said.

Patrick disappeared again.

Adele told Martin and Anna, "I'll be as quick as I can."

A moment later her telephone rang.

"Adele Buffington."

A deep male voice said, "It looks like I've had a little luck this morning at last. Maybe it isn't going to be one of those awful can't-get-anything-done days after all."

"Who is this, please?" Adele asked.

"Detective Sergeant Proffitt of the Indianapolis Police Department, ma'am."

"What is it that you want, Detective Sergeant?"

"When I came into work this morning I was assigned to investigate your break-in."

"Yes?"

"That means I need to arrange a time to talk to you. I tried to call you at home but your little girl seemed a bit sleepy and she didn't know where you were."

"She had a late night and I left before she got up."

"I tried you at home because I assumed that after what happened last night, you would be off work."

"I had a report that simply had to be finished."

"I see, ma'am." Proffitt paused before saying, "I am right that the guy last night roughed you up some?"

"A little." Adele stiffened, expecting a repeat of some of the exploratory questioning from the night before. But it didn't come.

Proffitt said, "Most folks find that kind of experience to be pretty disturbing."

"I can assure you," Adele said with some impatience, "I am just as human as the next person."

"So this report you needed to finish must have been urgent," Proffitt said.

After a moment, Adele said, "Please, Sergeant Proffitt, just when is it you wished to talk to me?"

"First thing I got this case, I noticed the description you gave of your intruder. Pretty unusual size of guy, is that right?" He spoke slowly, with southern inflections, and he seemed to take the ends of sentences extremely seriously.

"Yes."

"I went down and put the description through our computer. There aren't all that many men hereabouts who have the size you say this man had, so the computer turned up a fairly limited number of possibilities."

Pause. "Yes?"

"That assumes, of course, that the man who broke in has a record around here."

"Yes?"

"I thought the best thing to do would be for you to come downtown to have a look at our pictures. Would that be possible?"

Adele thought about her day, tried to remember what she had down in her appointment book. All she could think of was that she needed to go shopping.

Proffitt said, "We could go over details of what happened. I promise, I will do what I can to expedite your visit."

Expedite? "Oh. Right. All right."

"When can you get here, ma'am?"

Adele looked at her watch. "I'm in an important meeting now, but if I leave in a few minutes . . . Half an hour? Forty minutes?"

"That would be real helpful. Do you know your way around down here?"

"Yes. I used to be a probation officer."

"OK. You just ask for me at the information desk inside the front door. That's Detective Sergeant Proffitt."

When Adele hung up, she sighed.

Immediately, Anna said, "You are not going to duck out on us, Adele. We have a right to know certain things."

"I'll tell you *whatever* you want to know, Anna."

"What was stolen, then?"

"Nothing."

"Nothing at all?"

"The man seems to have come in just to copy a file. He didn't take anything."

"What file?" Martin asked.

"I don't know. But it was in A TO H, and when I get the chance I'll see if I can find anything out of place. Can you all do without that drawer till I get back? I've got to go down to look at some pictures at the police department."

"Do they have a suspect?" Martin asked.

"They have come up with some pictures from the description I gave them last night. That's what they want me to go downtown for now."

Anna asked, "Last night did this man hurt you or assault you or anything?"

"He was very emotionally worked up about something and he threatened me."

"Gosh," Martin said.

"He also expressed a very low opinion of social workers. And he was physically very large. I decided I had no choice but to let him do what he wanted to do."

"Is there any reason to think he'll come back?" Martin asked. "I mean, shouldn't we have some kind of alarm system on the windows and doors?"

"Willy mentioned security when he was here this morning."

"This is not the most salubrious area in the city, Adele," Martin said. "Should you have been working in the office alone at night?"

"Maybe we'll need to consider an office policy about that kind of thing."

Formally, Anna said, "I think we are long overdue for a meeting with Massa Hendricks about office security. Tina said that this man got in because the interview room window was unlocked. I mean, that's absolutely ridiculous!"

"The police seemed to think it was not locked, but we're not sure."

"Locked or not, it certainly wasn't secure," Anna said.

"Perhaps everyone could think through yesterday," Adele said, "about who you were with in the interview room and whether anyone had a chance to unlatch the window without your knowing. Give me a memo each, on my desk when I get back. And ask Tina to do the same."

"All right," Martin said.

"While we're writing things down," Anna said, "would you object if I prepared a report on office security?"

"Is this a special interest area of yours?"

"I have a friend or two who would know about this kind of thing. I think I could work out some measures that would be pretty constructive. For you and Mr. Hendricks to consider."

"All right. I'm perfectly happy to have a report like that and take it to Willy if the suggestions are good ones."

"They will be," Anna said.

"I'm also willing to have suggestions from the rest of you in this area," Adele said. "Whether you want to present them in a report form or not. Martin, could you make sure Tina knows about that, too?"

"Sure," Martin said.

Adele sat forward in her chair. "Now, will that do for the time being? I've told this cop I'll be downtown as soon as I can get there."

"Yes, of course," Martin said. Anna said nothing.

At that moment Tina McLarnon appeared beside Patrick in the office doorway. "Adele," she said, "I think you should come out and talk to this woman. She is saying some rather extraordinary things about her grandson."

6

WHEN Adele did finally leave the office, her car's sluggish acceleration reminded her that it was due for servicing. Overdue.

What was the list of little things to remember when she took it in? Heating fan didn't work. Maybe a fuse. And there seemed to be oil leaking, from somewhere. And . . . And . . .

Damn. There *was* something else.

She found a space in the Market Square lot. She sat in the car and thumbed through her appointment book. No way tomorrow. Probably not till the middle of next week. She wrote a note: "Car service." She got out and went across the street to police headquarters. She was forty minutes late.

As she stopped at the information counter in the center of the first-floor waiting area, Adele was approached by a slim, black-haired man of average height who was about thirty years old.

"Mrs. Buffington?"

"Buffington, but not Mrs.," Adele said. "I think of myself as Ms., if anything."

41

"Homer Proffitt, ma'am. Detective Sergeant." He proffered a hand.

Adele shook it. "I'm sorry to be late. Normally I run on time, but just as I was leaving something urgent came up."

"Lot of 'urgent' things in your life, Ms. Buffington."

"Yes."

"I'll try to take up as little of your time as possible. Come this way, OK?"

Proffitt turned and led Adele to an elevator behind the information desk.

They traveled to the fourth floor and walked a short distance from the elevator through a secured door to a room filled with desks. He led her to one with an inch-high stack of photographs on it.

"Have a seat," he said, gesturing to a straight-backed chair at the side of the desk.

"Thank you."

He settled himself and opened a large envelope. He withdrew a sheet of paper and gave it to her. "Could you just check that these details about you are correct?"

Adele read her name, profession, home and work addresses and phones, birth date, marital status, children.

"Yes, they are all correct," she said.

"That's a change," Proffitt said easily. "Johnny Wartman—the officer you talked to last night—he isn't real strong on the accuracy of his details."

"And are you?"

Proffitt smiled. "I try to be, ma'am."

"It's been a hundred years since anybody called me 'ma'am' seriously."

"You sure have aged real well."

Adele blinked, then smiled back.

Proffitt withdrew a second sheet from the envelope and glanced at it. "Johnny also seemed to think that your intruder abused you in ways that you were reluctant to tell him about."

"I told him essentially what happened. But your Johnny was quite eager to find some sexual content to the events. Does that make it a bigger case for him, or what?"

Proffitt ignored her question and asked, "Essentially?"

"Mm."

He waited for her.

She said, "The man touched my left breast and got me to look down so that he could flick my nose with his finger, as a joke."

"And you didn't tell Johnny?"

"I interpreted what the man did as a way of establishing his position of power rather than as something sexual."

"Uh huh."

"I didn't think it was important."

"I expect you were right."

"One thing we learn only too well dealing with children in hostile environments is that sexual abuse is usually about power and dominance, not sex."

"Uh huh," Proffitt said again. "Well, let's have a look at these guys, OK?"

"OK."

"You told Johnny that your intruder was about six eight, and something like twenty-five years old."

"I said in his mid-twenties."

"I've got a few pictures here I thought it would be a good thing for you to look through." He picked up the pile of photographs.

"It seems that there are quite a few people after all who fit my description," Adele said.

Proffitt said, "Well, what you got there is the guys six three and over between eighteen and forty."

"I can tell the difference between six eight and six three, Sergeant Proffitt."

"Well, I was just covering the chance that we got some of the heights wrong on our records," he said.

Adele studied the man's face.

It did not change expression.

She snorted gently. "Proffitt, you may talk like a hayseed," she said, "but you act like a slick son of a bitch."

He grinned. "Ma'am, from the likes of a sophisticated and professional lady like yourself, I think I take that as a compliment."

Adele picked up the stack of pictures.

"In my experience," Proffitt said, "people are more comfortable trying to place faces if nobody is watching over their shoulder, so I'm going to leave you for a while. Would you like a cup of coffee?"

"Is there tea?"

"Hot or cold?"

"Hot, with a bit of milk."

He nodded and left her.

Adele closed her eyes for a moment and tried to visualize the man she was about to try to identify.

When Proffitt returned carrying two cups, Adele was waiting for him.

"No luck, huh?"

"Do you say that for a special reason or are you pessimistic by nature?"

He passed her a cup of tea and a napkin, then sat in his chair. "Well, ma'am, I don't see as you've taken any pictures out of the pack and you've left the same picture on the top that I had there to begin with. Now we both know the one on the top isn't the guy."

"And why's that?"

"For a start he's the wrong color. And for a finish he's kind of in jail."

"I guess by having me look at his picture you were just covering the possibility that he escaped yesterday and was wearing a mask," Adele said.

"We get a whole lot less trouble in court if we're real careful about not seeming to plant images in identification witnesses' minds."

"It would be nice if everyone in your job were so scrupulous."

"Most of us are," Proffitt said.

"I guess I'll have to take your word for it."

"It's becoming so we can't hardly help it, the way these things are handled in court. But we also understand a lot more about the unreliability of identification than we used to. Believe me, nobody wants to pull the wrong guy."

"I was worried about looking at the pictures when I came here."

"Why's that?"

"In case I thought I recognized him, but wasn't sure."

"But in fact you're sure that none of them is our man."

"Yes."

Proffitt nodded several small nods. He said, "Of course, it would have been easier if you'd said, 'Here, this is him.' But it's quite interesting if a guy who'd break into your agency branch *isn't* on our files."

"I suppose it is."

Proffitt closed his eyes and tilted his head back as if to gaze at the ceiling. He said again, "Quite interesting." After a moment he looked back at Adele.

"He certainly stressed his distaste for social workers generally," she said.

"Did he now?" Proffitt made a face. "I didn't see that in Johnny's report."

"Maybe Johnny didn't write it down because there is nothing prurient about *distaste*."

"You think ol' Johnny's got a bit of a one-track mind, now don't you?"

Adele said nothing.

"Still, I expect this guy's not the first person who has said a bad word or two about social workers."

"I think it's fair to say that in some quarters social workers are not the most valued people in Hoosier society."

"Like the police."

"I guess."

"I hadn't thought about it before," Proffitt said, "but you folks probably get a lot of the same kind of prejudiced treatment that we get, as if everyone in the job is equal to our lowest common denominator."

"That sounds about right."

"Well, maybe you and I have us a basis for some common understanding, Ms. Buffington."

Adele said nothing.

Proffitt sat up and looked at her. "Which I think we're going to need if I'm going to find this fella. For sure, I'm going to have to count on you to give me the right direction to look in."

She smiled slightly. "I agree."

"Ma'am, do you mind if I say you seem pretty savvy about these things?"

"Thank you."

Proffitt waited, but when Adele did not continue, he smiled again. "Now I thought that that was a real good opportunity for you to tell me all about this private eye boyfriend you got."

"Is it important?"

He gestured to his case file and said, "Johnny thought so. I think maybe I better have a little chat with Johnny, about what we need in a case report and what we don't."

"There's a detailed book on reporting procedures, isn't there?"

Proffitt smiled more broadly than before. "I'll be damned," he said. "Now this time you have surprised me. How'd you know about that?"

"An old friend of mine wrote a version for people on night cover."

"And who would that be?"

"Leroy Powder. Of course he's been in Missing Persons for quite a while now."

"I know the gentleman by sight," Proffitt said. "But

anymore Missing Persons is out at 25th and Keystone with the Juvenile Branch, so I don't come across Lieutenant Powder very often."

"Uh huh."

Proffitt rocked his head. "Golly, you're one sharp person."

"Do they train hillbilly flannel in the Indianapolis Police Academy these days?" Adele asked. "Or is that just the touch of style you bring to the job?"

"I admit I started my law enforcement career a little south of Indianapolis."

"Whereabouts?"

"Evansville."

"How long have you been up here?"

"A little over three years."

"May I ask why you made the move?"

"Long-term career potential is better here."

"I see."

"But I've only been a detective again for about a month."

"So you're still getting the cases the other people don't want."

"Anybody's got to work into a new system. And don't dismiss what happened last night. It's not trivial," Proffitt said.

"It wasn't exactly a terrorist attack."

"A guy broke in, and he scared you pretty bad."

"Yes."

"You're not the easiest person to scare."

"No."

"Well, I feel society would be a little bit safer if we found this fella. Don't you?"

"Yes," Adele said.

Proffitt leaned back. "So how we going to do that?"

"When I get back, I will look through the A TO H drawer, to see if he put the file back in the wrong place or to see if I can find a folder that has its contents in a disturbed order. I've told my staff to leave the drawer alone."

Proffitt nodded. "I sure do wonder about the details of the case he photocopied." Then, "But it occurs to me to ask if you do locate the file whether you'll let me see more than just the name and address of the subject."

"There might be a problem about confidentiality."

"That's what I was thinking you might think." He considered. "But I know that whatever it says in the rules for our respective professions, what's right for the police is not always necessarily right for the people involved."

"No."

"Of course I'm not going to duck on anything important, but just let me say I'm also not going to go busting into anything that is best left alone."

"That is reassuring to know."

"OK." Proffitt opened a desk drawer and drew out a business card. On the back he wrote a number. "Any time you want to talk, any time day or night, these are where you can reach me. Whatever you want to talk about."

"Day or night?" Some surprise.

"I'm a new boy, ma'am. Eager to make my mark."

7

It was approaching noon as Adele made her way back to 34th Street. Catching sight of a public phone, she pulled up. The idea was to call home to try to catch Lucy, to ask her to do the shopping.

But the body of the telephone was askew, nearly pulled off its brackets. And it had no instrument to talk into.

Probably Lucy would have left home by now anyway.

Adele drove on, the shopping unresolved. Lucy sometimes called her "obsessed" by food, but domestic things didn't do themselves.

Like the washing.

Oooo, the washing. The plan had been to leave some things to soak this morning. Forgot.

Rats!

Adele pulled into the little churchyard next to the agency where the social workers parked.

She decided to try to reach Lucy from the office.

Then she thought about what would be waiting for her. Twelve-year-old Clyde. The A TO H drawer. Window memos. Security. Not to mention . . .

* * *

As Adele walked through the agency door, Tina came to her immediately.

"Give me a chance, Tina," Adele said.

"You'll never guess what happened."

Adele shook her head slowly, thinking, "What *now?*"

"A woman actually came into the office to *thank* us for something! The event of the month and you missed it."

"Tell."

"It was a neighbor of James Stepney's foster parents."

"James Stepney . . . Remind me."

"Little Diamond Jim, the eleven-year-old who stole the cuff links?"

"Ah ah ah." And the plastic "pearl" earrings and about a hundred other things. Whose mother joined in prosecuting him and refused to have him back home. Last March. Nearly a year ago.

"Well, James visits her."

"The neighbor woman?"

"That's right. They make a big deal out of it. Fix a time. Ring the bell. 'Come in for a cup of coffee, young man. Would you care for a cookie? Here, have a napkin.' Everything just so. She teaches him manners and he eats it up, if you'll pardon the—"

"I pardon."

"This woman, Mrs. Rideout, also says that James is perfectly happy with the Radzinskis, and she thought we ought to be told."

"That *is* nice," Adele said.

"Isn't it!" Tina said.

"Did you get her address, this Mrs. Rideout?"

Tina frowned. "No. Should I have?"

"It's potentially the kind of thing that Willy might be able to use. But if she's a neighbor of the Radzinskis, there shouldn't be a problem if he wants it."

"No."

"I'll make a note to tell him about it when he comes next week."

"He's still—?"

"I would advise you to have your records up to date, yes."

"All right," Tina said. "And now what say I update you on what you thought I was going to talk to you about when you came in the door."

Adele smiled, acknowledging Tina's correct reading of her expectation. Details about Clyde, the sexually active grandson.

They went to Adele's office.

Tina said, "I called Frances Tounley at Welfare about this child. These children, since we're talking about the three neighbor girls, too."

"Did you explain to Grandma that by law in this state we're obliged to report what she told us either to Welfare or the police?"

"Yes. It didn't bother her. She just wants it sorted out."

"And her precious Clyde saved from corruption."

"Yes," Tina said.

"I shouldn't be glib about it," Adele said. "But it seems so . . . oh, I don't know. What do you think? How accurate is Grandma's version of events going to be?"

"Honestly, at this point I can't tell," Tina said.

"What kind of kids copulate where a comparatively immobile grandmother can watch without their knowing?"

"Young ones, it would seem." Tina shrugged. "I don't know whether you agree, but I told Frances that I'd like to go along when the Welfare case worker visits the house. It's our referral, and it certainly has the potential to be a long-termer."

"That's fine. If you have the time."

"My records aren't *that* bad."

"Who's getting the case?"

"Frances has given it to Brenda Weekes."

"Oh, she'll get things sorted out," Adele said.

"I know she's a bit direct at times," Tina said.

"To put it mildly."

"But I get along well enough with Brenda," Tina said. "We're meeting after lunch and she's seeing that the boy will be at home."

"Good," Adele said.

Tina paused, then said, "Adele, we were due to review my cases this morning. Do you want to postpone, or do you want to do it this afternoon?"

"Is there anything that can't wait?"

"Not really."

Adele looked in her appointment book. "How about next Monday? Elevenish?"

"That's good by me."

"Unless Clyde goes on a rampage or something."

"I'm rather looking forward to meeting this young man," Tina said. Then, "How were the police?"

"Not very dramatic. I must have looked at fifty pictures, but none of them was *him*."

"Do you think they'll find the guy?"

"I don't have any idea. They've certainly assigned the case to a strange man. He presents as a hick and talks so slowly that you can go out for a cup of tea and come back before he gets to the end of a sentence. But underneath the cowpat exterior, he seems pretty sharp."

"Well, maybe they will."

"Maybe." Then, "Are things all right with you, Tina? Personally, I mean."

"Much as ever."

"How is George?"

"Increasingly George-like. I'm sorry. I don't mean to be uncommunicative, but as the man is almost impossible to talk to, it seems pretty appropriate."

"Are you still seeing your musician?"

"Only whenever I get a chance."

Tina was in her late twenties and the musician was the current relief from the throes of an on-again, off-again marriage that had taken place abruptly after the sudden end of an intense relationship within the office.

"Oh, to be young and tempestuous," Adele said. "Honestly, I don't know how you have the energy."

"It doesn't take much," Tina said. "I don't get to see Harry very often."

"Musicians' lives are bound to be uncertain."

"Musicians' mistresses' lives are bound to be even more uncertain. Especially a mistress who is not just 'the other woman' but 'the other other woman.'"

Adele smiled in response, as she was meant to.

"So if we get any cases that require night visits, keep me in mind. I'm usually available."

"Before you go, did you get the message about the interview room?"

"We all left memos," Tina said.

Adele found the memos. "Thanks."

"But I haven't been in the interview room all week and I don't think anybody else remembered much that was helpful."

"We can but try."

"Patrick was in there yesterday at lunchtime. As ever. He's in there now, writing his novel or whatever it is that he writes."

"I've asked everybody else. I suppose I should ask him, too."

"He'll feel left out if you don't."

"Poor old Patrick."

"Who would be young again?" Tina asked. She rose and left the office.

Patrick Cheese sat at the table in the interview room bent over a notebook. It was a thick spiral pad, and the page Adele could see was covered with tiny writing.

Patrick was surrounded by food containers.

"How many people are you feeding in here, Pat?" Adele asked.

Surprised, he jerked up and slammed his notebook shut. "Oh. It's only you."

"Yes, *only* me. The story of my life. The most handsome and exciting single man in the office and all he says is, 'Only you.' It's enough to make a grown woman cry."

"It's not like that. I just . . . Well, it isn't."

"Anna is at her desk, on the telephone."

Patrick blushed.

"I'll be talking to her in a minute. Do you have any message you want me to give her?"

"Of course not," he said.

Naughty, Adele thought. And undisciplined. And unkind. Must be feeling the fatigue. Oh, well.

She said, "Pat, when you were in this room yesterday, you didn't open the window, did you?"

"I didn't open it, Adele. I never do. And I've tried hard to remember if I saw anybody else, or anything about the window at all, but I can't remember a thing."

"OK."

"I don't know who among the others used the room," he said. Then, "Anna may have."

Which meant Anna certainly had, since Patrick kept track of Anna Pike's every movement.

"Yes, she did," Adele said. "I've had a look through the memos they all gave me."

"Oh."

Adele walked to the window and examined the catch and the frame. They were a bit loose but appeared to fit well enough.

She opened the catch. Tension from the slightly warped window frame opened a gap.

Maybe it just hadn't been locked. Stupid, but certainly possible. Also stupid not to have storm windows.

Ah, well.

"Thanks, Pat." She moved to leave.

"Adele?" Patrick asked.

"Yes?"

"Oh, never mind."

"What is it?"

"Well, if . . . if you really are about to speak to Anna . . ."

"Yes?"

"Maybe, if it's easy, could you tell her that I'll be down at Ike and Jonesy's tonight. I mean, don't tell her that I told you to tell her. But if it's easy to say . . ."

"Wouldn't it be better to ask her yourself?"

"If you don't want to, that's perfectly all right. I'll understand. Honest."

Anna Pike sat studying a case file. Her face, in repose, formed a frown.

Adele pulled a nearby chair to Anna's desk and sat down.

Without looking up, Anna said, "I'll be with you in a moment."

"I don't know why you don't give Patrick a chance," Adele said. "He's such a nice young man."

After the moment Anna sat back. "*Nice* is a busman's holiday for me, Adele. Being *nice* is part of the job around here. I am *nice* to clients. I am *nice* when I talk to other agencies. I am even *nice* to colleagues when I have to be."

Anna looked at Adele.

Adele looked back.

"So I prefer my men to be absolutely awful."

"And do you find many that fit the bill?"

"Absolute oodles. What can I do for you, boss?"

"Your memo says you talked to some clients yesterday in the interview room, but it's short on details."

"I talked to two families. Ron Snyder and that idiot common-law wife of his, Silly Sarah. And I saw little Jason Mason and his hoity-toity stepmother."

"Did you leave either group in the interview room

alone? Like, while you went to get a file or look something up, or something."

"I left both, briefly."

"What time did you see them?"

"Ron and Silly Sarah, about eleven-fifteen. Jason and"—snottily—"Felicia at two."

"Are either of the cases contentious?"

"I thought about it," Anna said, pulling at the flesh on her neck, "and they shouldn't be. Ron came in wanting help getting better access to his daughter. He was married—actually married—about fifteen years ago. Although he's had this string of women he's called his missus, he says with Sarah it's permanent, and there is the baby so . . ."

"Jason Mason is the autistic one."

"With the self-centered self-indulgent self-obsessed self-selfed mother."

"Considered extremely beautiful, if I recall."

"Yes," Anna said icily. "*Jason* is absolutely gorgeous."

"So what did Felicia Mason want?"

"What does she ever want? Somebody else to pay for a full-time Jason-minder so that she can spend more time in the beauty parlor. You know what she said to me? She said that she was emotionally very fragile yesterday because she found a 'pre-crow's-foot line' next to her left eye. She said that, she really did."

"Hmmm," Adele said, considering. But she dismissed both cases as unlikely to have inspired the violent anti-social work feelings so clearly expressed by the intruder. She stood up.

"That it?"

"For the moment," Adele said. "Except, do you ever go to a place called Ike and Jonesy's?"

Anna tried to unravel the intention of the question. Failing, she answered, "Sometimes. Not lately. Why?"

"I've heard it's pretty lively. I was thinking about taking Al there tomorrow night. Tell you what—as our resident expert on social life, what say you check it out for me tonight and report back."

Anna remained puzzled. She said, "It's a singles bar. A relatively respectable one."

"Well, Al and I are both single."

Martin Cretney was not in the office. At lunch, Adele supposed. And the idea of lunch led her to consider whether she was hungry herself.

But even if she was, shouldn't she get on with studying A TO H?

Or, if she hurried, would there be time to do the shopping and take it home to get the frozen things in the freezer?

Just as she opted for the files, her phone rang.

"Adele Buffington."

"Hah," Al said. "I bet myself you'd be there. You should be out having lunch. Good nourishment is vital to keep your energy level up and fight stress."

"Yes, Mother," Adele said.

"It's not that I disapprove of Anna being ambitious," Adele said. "In fact, I positively do approve."

"What is it then?" Al asked.

"I just wish she would be ambitious more subtly. If she would say, 'Hope you're feeling all right, Adele,' before she used the break-in as a chance for a leg up with Willy. A report on office security indeed. If security were what she was interested in, she could make her suggestions verbally in thirty seconds."

Al stared into his chili bowl. He counted the beans.

"All right, sixty seconds," Adele said, by way of acknowledging his silent comment that she was letting Anna irritate her too much.

"How much of this is because you still don't like the way Willy landed her on you?"

"Some, I suppose."

Al waited for her.

"Willy knows I wouldn't have hired her. But that's Willy for you."

"Likes his diamonds rough?"

"What's galling is that she's totally different with clients. She talks about them as if she loathes them, but she talks *to* them with as much sympathy and concern as you could ask for."

"Sounds like a girl with problems," Al said.

Adele smiled to acknowledge that her "nice man" was social-working the social worker.

Then she said, "It's been a long time since we had lunch together. It's good. Thank you." She reached across the table and squeezed his hand.

"You made me feel guilty about how long it's been since I've been around," Al said. He was a substantial man in his middle forties. "I can hardly expect you to continue being my special friend if I don't make a bit of an effort."

"Right," Adele said. Remembering Anna's favorite word, "*Absolutely* right."

"Besides, one of my cases is on hold just at the moment. The suspected cashier is off sick. Can I have one of your squid?"

They rarely talked about their respective work, a relationship rule. Apart from anything else, Adele often had too much and Albert too little.

"For three beans and a spoonful of juice."

The deal was struck.

"By the way," Al said, "Lucy's Fritz is rich."

"Rich?"

"Unless there is more than one Fritz Kory Goodhew from Milwaukee in the sociology department. And the sociology department says there isn't."

"How did you get that information out of them?"

"Don't ask me too many questions, sunshine."

Adele thought. "I thought she said he was from Minnesota."

"Minnesota, Wisconsin. They're all the same up there. Yogurt and skis."

"They told you he was rich? Is that what's replaced grade point averages?"

"My contact, a vibrant petite blonde with a great body, said, 'You know who he is, don't you?' I played dumb. They love that. And then she said, 'Frozen food. Does that give you a clue?' and I played cool and said, 'Nope.' And then she said, 'Are you really trying to recruit sociology graduates for AT&T?' and I said I was actually a private detective and she said, 'Pull the other one,' and I said, 'It will be my pleasure but shouldn't we go someplace more private.' And she giggled and I said, 'You must be very sharp; nobody has ever seen through me before yet you got it like I was a piece of Saran Wrap,' and she said, 'Like a tack, and I'm vibrant, petite and blonde too.' "

"What about the great body?"

"I made that up."

"So what frozen food?"

"They specialize in supplying restaurants, hotels and so on. Catering packages. And they *are* big—all over the Midwest—and Daddy owns it. Gunter Goodhew."

"Oh."

"Can't tell you anything much else about the kid. Except that he's twenty-four, went to the University of Wisconsin and, at least on the application form, didn't admit to being already married."

"Why's he in Indianapolis: I mean, why grad school here?"

"Can't tell you. Yet."

8

WHEN Adele returned to the office she walked into a fight.

A thin man in his fifties with a straggly gray beard leaned forward to put his weight on the handle of a wooden cane. He and Anna Pike were almost nose-to-nose. They were shouting at each other.

"Why don't you just take a hike!" Anna said.

"Some fucking community service," the man said.

"You think you can stroll in off the street and *demand* things?" Anna said. "She-it! Not around here you can't. Join the real world, Jack, or get out."

Patrick hovered behind Anna with all the resolution of a moth. He was bigger physically than either of the combatants, but he was totally unable to affect events. No one else was in the office.

"I will *not* talk to *you*," the man said. "When I want the engineer no way am I going to settle for the oily rag."

"I am nobody's fucking oily rag!"

"And I'm *certainly* not going to settle for the snot on the oily rag!"

The pair stared and glared as they paused for breath and inspiration.

In the moment, Adele stepped forward, touching their shoulders. "Ssshh" she said. "The baby's sleeping!"

For no apparent reason this absurdity instantly gained the attention of both Anna and the man. Each stepped back and looked around.

Adele stepped into the gap. She faced Anna and pointed to her desk. "Sit down, Ms. Pike."

"An absolute nut case," Anna said. She retreated to her desk. "An absolute fucking nutter."

Adele turned to the man. She said, "Either take a seat in the interview room over there or leave. Now."

"Take me to the man in charge," he said.

"I'm the man in charge," Adele said.

"I should have known." He blew his nose into a dirty handkerchief. Then he went to the interview room.

Finally Adele turned to Patrick. "What got this started?"

Anna turned and began to speak.

Adele pointed a finger at her and said, "I asked Patrick."

Anna shrugged and turned away.

"Pat?"

Uncomfortably, Patrick said, "This guy came in and I asked what he wanted and he said he came to see whoever was in charge and that it was important. Anna was the only person here." He looked down and blushed. "Apart from me, of course."

"What happened?"

"I took him over to Anna and next thing *I* knew he was shouting at her. You know the kind of people we get in here sometimes. It wasn't Anna's fault, Adele, honest."

As Adele entered the interview room the man was standing by the window. He turned and lifted the cane and put the head between them. It was a gesture to forestall criticism.

The head was carved into a likeness of William Shake-speare.

The man said, "Despite what that stuck-up little bitch may have said, I'm not a lunatic."

"In that case, what are you?"

"My name is King Smith," the man said. "I've become aware of something very weird. I walk by the 'child welfare' signs in your window every day of my life, so I thought I'd give you a chance to put up or shut up."

"That's very kind of you, Mr. Smith."

"Call me King. Everybody calls me King."

"Well, you can call me the exception, Mr. Smith."

"Why are you people so damn argumentative?"

"Mr. Smith, my name is Adele Buffington. What say we bypass further pleasantries and get on with whatever it was that brought you here."

Smith considered, almost smiled, and said, "All right."

"You said something was weird."

"Yeah, well . . ."

"Try the beginning," Adele said, with as much "niceness" in her voice as she could muster. She sat down.

So did Smith.

"I have a neighbor," he said. "A woman, in an apartment across the hall from me. It's an awful place we live in, dirty and old, and it's only the bug spit that holds it together."

Smith paused for Adele to react.

She waited for him.

"But it's cheap, which is why anyone would live there."

"Yes?"

"My neighbor's name is Donna. I don't know her well, but she was already living there when I moved in about seven months ago. She has two kids, twins, both little girls. They look about five to me, but I don't know that much about kids, never having been careless enough to spawn one myself."

Adele waited.

"The kids have something wrong with them."

"What?"

"The heads are a little funny-shaped. I don't know exactly. Mongoloid maybe."

Down's syndrome? "All right."

"Donna has been living off some man. All I know are a few details. She was supposed to be due to inherit some money from somewhere. The man is some kind of lawyer and he's been giving her advances on it and she's used the money to fix her apartment up and buy food and clothes for the kids."

"Uh huh," Adele said.

"But none of them ever go out."

Adele frowned. "They stay in the apartment?"

Smith nodded and said, "Donna doesn't shop for food—she orders it by phone and has it delivered. And I think the clothes come by mail, too."

Deliberately, "It does sound a bit disquieting."

Smith leaned back and paused, having her attention. Then, "I haven't got to the bad part yet."

"Well get to it."

"I'm around my own place a lot." A look of defiance. "I am a writer. A playwright, in fact."

"Yes?"

"The point is that normally I work most of the day, except for a long walk. Which is why I pass your door regularly."

"I see."

"I spend most of my time in my living room. What I am saying is that, without trying to, I keep pretty good track of what happens at Donna's. Ours are the only apartments on the top floor of the building. So any sounds that aren't mine must be hers. So I *know* they never go out and that almost nobody comes to visit them. They get food deliveries and Donna goes downstairs to get the mail, but otherwise I hear the kids playing or the television or whatever."

"What about this man who advances her money?"

"Somebody comes on a Monday night. Up the stairs, to the door, opens it by key, goes in. He stays about an hour or an hour and a half. But that's it."

"Regularly, once a week?"

"Every Monday. But occasionally on other days, too."

"The father of the children?"

"I don't know."

"But you've talked to Donna?"

"For the first time, on Tuesday."

"Tuesday as in the day before yesterday?"

"The first time that was more than a 'Good morning.' Yes."

"After seven months of being neighbors?"

"I'm not going to apologize."

"It's a little unfriendly, isn't it?"

"I am devoted to my work," King Smith said. "It's my whole life. I am perfectly happy to make acquaintances, but I *don't* like to become involved with neighbors in an apartment building. They're too close if something goes wrong between you."

"It's one attitude."

"That's not to say that I was completely unaware of them, as I've said. But it wasn't, you know, my business."

"But then it became your business."

"Tuesday about nine Donna came to my door to borrow a cup of sugar. I don't use sugar, and I was about to close the door when she said flour would do instead. She just, well, stood there."

Smith opened his eyes wide and gave Adele the impression that he was mimicking what Donna had looked like.

"And?"

"I thought about it and then I invited her in. She walked in and went straight to my chair and sat down and she started to cry." He snorted. "Women and their tears!"

"What did you do?"

"I got her a cup of flour and put it on the desk next to her, but she didn't seem very interested."

"And?"

"Finally she stopped crying and started talking, which is how it all came out. I mean about this money she was supposed to inherit and this guy giving her advances on it."

"But something had happened?" Adele said.

"The night before the guy made his regular visit, but instead of giving her money he told her he was calling in all the advances. Donna didn't know what to do. She said she thought he had been giving her this money, advancing it, only now he was saying it was all loans and that he couldn't wait anymore for this inheritance to come through and he was calling the loans in."

"What did you tell her?"

"I said she should go to Welfare if she didn't have any money to eat, but she said she couldn't. That the guy had been to Welfare to tell them about the inheritance and that he was providing her money."

"That sounds very peculiar," Adele said.

"I'm only telling you what Donna said. I have a *very* good memory for conversations. It's an invaluable help in my work."

"All right."

"Then I told her she should go to a lawyer—to find out about this inheritance and what it was really all about."

"What was her reaction to that?"

"She didn't like it. I . . . I had the feeling that it was a little beyond what she felt she was capable of doing. I think Donna is not real bright. A nice thing, straightforward, but not well endowed upstairs. Or worldly-wise. Then I said she should go to the police, but that just got her upset again. Very, very upset."

"And this was Tuesday night?"

"Yes."

"What happened then?"

"I gave her a little money."

"Oh."

"Well, this guy hadn't given her anything," King Smith said. "I felt sorry for her. I . . . liked her. As a character study."

"And what happened then?"

"She was grateful for the cash and seemed to think that I would want something for it."

"And did you?"

"That question is beneath contempt," Smith said.

"If you say so, Mr. Smith," Adele said.

"Anyway, at that point Donna went back to her apartment. She said it was to see that the girls were all right and she would come back. I waited. She didn't come."

"What did you do?"

"Nothing. I let it go."

"So what did you do yesterday?"

"I worked as usual, but then I heard steps on the stairs. I got up and opened my door a crack in time to see a short guy going into Donna's apartment."

"Was he the man who visited her every Monday?"

"I don't know," Smith said. "I never saw him."

"In seven months?"

"I am not nosy about people I am not involved with."

"Yes. All right."

"He was in there a long time, more than two hours. But in the circumstances, I listened for him, and when I heard him come out I went onto the landing, as if I was going somewhere, but he was already on the stairs and Donna's door was closed."

"So you didn't get another look?"

"No."

"While he was in Donna's apartment did you hear anything?"

"I heard her cry for a while," Smith said quietly.

"Oh."

"But it wasn't for long. And she stopped quite a while before the guy left."

"Did you hear the children?"

King Smith thought for a moment. "Now you mention it, I didn't."

"So what happened then?"

"After I heard the guy leave the building, I knocked on Donna's door."

"And?"

"She would talk to me only through the chain. She said she was all right. She said that the man she owed the money to was going to find someplace that she could work to pay off her debts."

"Oh."

"I told her that the whole thing sounded funny to me and that I thought she should get help. I even offered to help her myself."

"What did she say?"

"She thanked me, but said she was going to work it out on her own." Smith paused, then said, "She seemed, well, odd. There was something about her."

Adele asked, "Could she have been on drugs of some kind?"

King Smith froze.

"I never thought of that."

"So you think it's possible."

He considered. "Possible."

"And," Adele said, "this 'lawyer' might have been bringing Donna something besides money on a Monday night."

"I suppose."

"Which might help explain why she was so upset when he didn't give her the money the day before and why she was so grateful when you gave her some cash yourself."

"I never even thought."

Adele allowed herself to say, "It could be that Donna is not the only one in your building who is a little unworldly from staying at home too much."

"It could be," Smith said, "that you are a little smarter than you look."

"What did you do next?"

"I asked Donna how she was doing for money now. She thought it was a hint and she left me at the door to get money to pay back what I had given her the day before. She passed it through the crack and then she closed the door. I didn't know what to do."

"What did you do?"

"I thought about it."

"And?"

"This morning I knocked on her door again. I had decided to tell her that I was going to go to tell somebody about it all unless she could give me a good reason not to."

"And?"

"They were gone."

"Gone?"

"The door was open. That is, unlocked. When there was no answer, I tried the knob. And I went in. I can tell you, I was very worried about what I was going to find."

"What did you expect to find?"

"I hadn't heard anybody leave. I was afraid she'd killed herself and the kids, she was so upset when she talked to me on Tuesday. Upset, as in desperate. But when I went in there was nothing. It looked like they had packed up things like clothes and left things like dishes and furniture."

"What do you think happened?"

"I don't know. But I decided I had to tell someone."

"I agree."

"It was either you people or the cops. I decided on

you because of that damn stuff in the window about how you deal with child welfare. It seemed to me that these kids weren't getting much welfare if they were being kept at home all the time with nobody but their mother. But when I came in and had to talk to that hatchet-brained child who was so rude to me, I regretted that I hadn't gone to the cops. So I was rude back."

"So I heard."

"Why do you employ someone like that?"

"Anna is a fine young social worker, capable of exceptional perception and delicacy, especially when she is dealing with children."

"Some kind of arrested development so she can't deal with adults, huh?"

"It seems to me that by the time I arrived on the scene you were dishing out at least as much as was being thrown at you."

"Quite possibly. I'm very sensitive."

"Certainly more than you seemed to be at first sight."

"Am I supposed to thank you for that?"

"Instead, why don't you tell me what else you know about Donna."

"Like what?"

"Does she have a last name, for instance?"

"East."

9

On his way out King Smith stopped in front of Anna Pike's desk. Anna was on the telephone.

"Hey, snotty rag," Smith said. "To my amazement I've had a constructive talk with your engineer, and I just wanted to say if you're premenstrual or something and that's what made you so obnoxious, I accept your apology."

He pivoted on Shakespeare's head and headed for the door.

Anna Pike sat mouth open and without riposte.

The person on the other end of the phone said, "Anna? Anna?"

Anna Pike said, "Let me call you back," and hung up. But Smith was gone.

As Adele passed from the interview room to her office, she said, "Anna, come in here a minute, please."

Anna looked toward Adele and then toward the door. She rose from her desk and went into Adele's office. Adele closed the door behind her.

Anna turned and squinted defensively. She said, "He walked in looking for trouble. I think the best way to deal with people like that is to show them they can't intimidate you."

"You lost control," Adele said.

"It kind of depends how—"

"Shut up."

Anna stopped.

"I didn't hire you, but I can go a long way toward firing you." Emphasizing each word, Adele said, "Anna, if you *ever* lose your temper with a member of the public like that again, you're out of here. Gone. Do I make myself clear? *Absolutely* clear?"

Anna said nothing.

"Must I say it again, or will your resignation be on my desk by the end of the afternoon?"

"You've made yourself clear."

"Good."

And then Anna said, "You're absolutely right. I shouldn't lose my temper, no matter how crazy the people who come in here are."

Adele hesitated. The impulse to criticize "crazy" was stilled by sheer surprise at the sudden apology.

Anna said, "If you've got the jerk-off's address I'll even go and apologize to him."

When Anna was gone, Adele sat at her desk and tried to gather her thoughts. Before sorting out what social work she should be doing, she called home, on the slight chance that Lucy would be there.

Of course, she wasn't.

Then Adele called Frances Tounley at Welfare, to talk about Donna East. But Tounley was not at her desk. Rather than speak to anyone else, Adele decided she would call back later.

She checked her watch. Tina and Welfare's Brenda Weekes would be meeting Clyde the grandson.

My God, it all happens at once.

Adele thought again about Donna East. There was no question that it had to be followed up. If the two children *never* went out . . .

She took some paper and made notes on her memory of the conversation with King Smith.

Indiana law says that possible abuse must be reported either to Welfare or to the police.

Thinking about the police, Adele decided to call a friend at the Indianapolis Police Department.

"Missing Persons," a female voice said. "Sergeant Fleetwood."

"May I speak to Lieutenant Powder, please?"

"He's not in the office. I would be happy to help you if I can."

It was a practiced response, but Adele felt a tone of truth about the offer. Missing Persons had become one of the most effective of the police departments in the city and one of the best such units in the country. Where in other places the police delayed searches for older children and adults until they'd been gone for some time, in Indianapolis procedures began as soon as someone notified the department.

Adele said, "It's Roy Powder that I really want to speak to, Sergeant Fleetwood. Will he be back later?"

"He won't, I'm afraid. Is this a Missing Persons matter or are you a friend?"

"My name's Adele Buffington. I am an old friend, but it's about business."

Fleetwood repeated the name. "Ah, yes," she said with recognition. "Roy's mentioned you."

"I'm flattered. I haven't spoken to him for quite a while."

"Well, Powder's on an extended leave of absence."

"Leroy Powder? On leave?"

Sergeant Fleetwood laughed. "You obviously do know the gentleman."

"But it sure sounds like I am out of touch."

"I can give you his home number, if you don't have it. His son, Ricky, is living there and would probably be able to tell you exactly where Roy is and whether you can contact him."

"Roy on leave *and* Ricky living at his house? I don't think I can take all this in."

"Oh, yes. They're thick as thieves now. In fact, Roy may well be doing some kind of legwork getting Ricky started in business."

"It makes sense that he isn't just lying on a beach."

"That's true," Fleetwood said. Then, "Look, are you sure it's nothing I could help you with?"

Adele considered. She asked, "Are you the Sergeant Fleetwood on the missing persons television program?"

"That's right."

"Well, I'm a social worker with the Hendricks Agency."

"I've heard of it," Fleetwood said.

"I've just been told quite a puzzling story."

Adele explained the facts King Smith had given her about Donna East and the family's sudden departure.

"If your source is sound," Fleetwood said, "then it does sound like something's not right."

"This neighbor just walked in off the street, so I don't know whether he's reliable or not. But I intend to go to the address this afternoon, and I hope that will give me a better sense of what the situation is."

"OK," Fleetwood said. "And what exactly was it that you were thinking of asking Roy to do?"

"If Donna and the children have gone off with this 'lawyer' it's not that they're exactly missing," Adele said. "But I hoped that Roy would have been willing to check police files for me, if I get some more details. Like who the lawyer is, for instance—if I can get his name."

"I'll be happy to do whatever I can to help," Fleetwood said. "When you have more information, why don't you try me on the things you might have asked Roy. All right?"

"That is a spectacularly generous offer, Sergeant Fleetwood. Thank you."

"Carollee, please. I can certainly start by seeing if there's anything on a Donna East in her early twenties who has two children."

Adele was on her way out of the office when Anna called to her.

"What is it, Anna?"

"I need my Garmsons' file. Has the embargo on the A TO H drawer been lifted or does Essie Garmson endure yet another day of emotional victimization?"

"Shit!" Adele said. "The A TO H files."

"Exactly."

"I haven't been through them yet. With everything that's been happening, last night seems a year ago."

Anna looked at her without sympathy.

Adele said, "I'll go through them now."

"So kind," Anna said. She returned to the work on her desk.

Adele moved to the filing cabinets. She opened the file drawer and first leafed through the tags to see whether the cases were in alphabetical order.

They were.

Then she pulled the first file in the drawer and opened it to determine whether the documents inside were organized in a normal sort of way.

The seventh file she examined appeared to be disturbed.

The discovery was exciting.

The temptation to close the drawer and leave the office was real, but the need for method held sway. Adele continued, folder by folder, through the contents of the drawer. Within minutes a second case record, with pages upside down, showed that the scrupulousness had been justified.

The exhilaration of discovery vanished.

Near the end of the drawer she found a third file with records in a seemingly senseless order, with visit details buried in a profusion of correspondence.

With the three case files in a pile, Adele closed the drawer and turned to Anna. But before she could speak, Martin Cretney rushed into the office.

"Adele! Adele!" he said, as he hurried to where Adele stood at the filing cabinet. He carried a newspaper.

"What?"

"Look at this! Look at this!"

On the closest desk Martin spread the front page of an early edition of the *Indianapolis News.* He pointed to a small article near the bottom.

It said that the unidentified body of a man had been found on Monument Circle shortly after dawn. He appeared to have been murdered. Police had found a note pinned to the victim's jacket, which read, "Hands off, social workers!" A homicide investigation had been opened. There were no further details.

"Oh, wonderful," Adele said, bending over the article, reading it again. The venom of the intruder the night before, her fear, came back. "They're killing us now," she said.

10

ADELE stayed in the office, sharing the general agitation. It was as if the murder were somehow personal, even though none of them knew quite what "Hands off, social workers!" might mean.

Only Anna appeared resistant to the unease. "Look at it," she said. "Maybe it's a typo."

"What do you mean?" Martin said.

"Maybe the actual note didn't have the comma. That way it reads, 'Hands off social workers!' So the dead guy was someone who was picking on one of us and he was killed by a grateful client."

No one even smiled.

"What are you all so grim about?" Anna persisted. "You don't know any facts."

Patrick said vaguely, "We don't know who it was or why."

"It's about time we found out then," Martin said. "Adele, is there anyone you can call?"

"I'll try," she said.

She went to her office. She dialed Carollee Fleetwood, but the number was busy.

She tried Homer Proffitt. To her surprise he was at his telephone at police headquarters.

"Yes, ma'am," he said. "What can I do for you?"

"I've just been shown an article in the *News* about a man who was found dead this morning with a note pinned to his body about social workers. Is that true?"

Proffitt paused. Then, "Yes, ma'am, it is."

"Do you know anything about it?"

"As it happens I had lunch with one of the fellas on the team and he spoke about the case. What is it that you wanted to know?"

"Was the text of the note that was printed in the newspaper the exact text that was on the note?"

"What was in the newspaper, ma'am?"

"It said the note read hands off comma social workers exclamation mark."

"I see."

"Is that what the note actually said?"

"Not quite, ma'am. I don't know about the punctuation, but the words were, 'Hands off social fucking workers.'"

"Oh."

"Excuse the French, ma'am."

"I was just wanting to confirm that the message was anti-social work."

"I think it's safe to say it was."

"Well," Adele said, unsure quite what else she wanted, "my people here are pretty disturbed by the story. Can you tell me any more about it?

"May I speculate that you think that the break-in at your office last night might be related to the murder?"

Adele hadn't been calm enough to make the connection consciously. But now that he put it into words . . .

"Ma'am?"

"Yes," she said. "That's what I was worried about."

"Well, ma'am, I kind of had the same thought, once I

heard about the homicide. Which is why I made a point
of having lunch with the particular officer I did."

"Are . . . Will you be working on that case, too?"

"No, not at the moment," Proffitt said. "They wouldn't
give something that juicy to a new boy. But I intend to
liaise since there may be a connection."

"The paper says the body hasn't been identified."

"Well . . ."

"So it has?"

"The body had a wallet with papers for a Brian Wampler."

"Oh, my good God!" Adele said.

"Does that name mean something to you, ma'am?"

Suddenly breathing very quickly she said, "Brian
Wampler used to be a social worker in this office."

"You don't say," Proffitt said slowly.

Adele suddenly visualized him at the other end of the
line, head back, eyes raised but closed, in thought.

"He left us about four months ago, but he worked
here for, oh, several years."

Forcefully, Proffitt said, "I will go and have a little talk
with the detective in charge of the case right now. Will
you be there? Are you at your office?"

"I . . . Yes. Yes. I'll be here."

"I'll call you back."

Adele hung the telephone up slowly. She lifted her
eyes to the ceiling. She blinked several times.

She rose from her desk and went back into the general office.

Anna said, "Something's wrong, isn't it?"

Adele said, "They think it was Brian."

"Brian?" Martin asked.

"Brian Wampler."

Martin said, "Murdered? Brian?"

"Yes."

Everyone remained still, absorbing the information.

Everyone but Anna, Wampler's replacement, had known him.

"Are they sure?" Martin Cretney asked.

"I spoke to the detective who's working on our break-in," Adele said. "He says the body had a wallet with ID in it."

"But the newspaper says it was unidentified."

"Sergeant Proffitt says the identification has not been made 'positively.' I don't know what that's supposed to mean. But it had Brian's ID."

"Jesus!" Martin said. "Brian was so . . . so vital." Then, "It's going to hit Tina pretty hard."

"Yes," Adele said. She looked at her watch, wondering if she could estimate when Tina would return.

For an extended period of time Tina had been Brian's girlfriend. Until they fought about his other women, and he dropped her for Janine, the typist/receptionist before Patrick. Within weeks Tina had gotten herself married.

Wampler's treatment of Janine had caused *her* to quit a job she was otherwise perfectly happy in. His continued presence in the office was one of the reasons a male typist/receptionist had been hired. And then he quit social work abruptly. *And* got married.

"What's Brian's wife's name?" Martin asked.

"Denise, I think," Adele said.

"What should we do?" Martin asked.

"I think . . . ," Adele began. And then she didn't know what she thought. "I don't know what I think," she said.

"Is it *possible* that it's not him?" Martin asked. "I mean, whoever it is could have stolen Brian's wallet."

Adele thought immediately of the note on the body that had referred to social workers. But she said, "I suppose it's possible."

"You don't think it's some lunatic who's going to become a Jack the Ripper of social workers, do you?" Anna asked. "Or a Jill the Ripper."

"I think it's a bit of a jump to go from one murder to an epidemic," Adele said. "Which isn't to say it isn't worrying."

"Poor Denise," Martin said. "How long had they been married?"

"A little under four months," Adele said.

Adele's telephone rang. She left the group to answer it.

It was Homer Proffitt. "I'm sorry to trouble you, Ms. Buffington, but do you think you could come downtown again? We would like you to have a shot at identifying the body."

"At . . . ?"

"I wouldn't ask if I didn't think it would serve some purpose."

"All right."

"Can you come now?"

"I guess so. Yes."

"I'll meet you where I met you before."

"All right."

When Adele came back from her office, everyone was staring at her.

"You look absolutely awful," Anna said.

Proffitt said, "You were very prompt."

"No point in delaying."

"Did you get here all right?"

Adele frowned.

Proffitt said, "The news must have been a shock. I was asking whether it made driving harder."

"It didn't make it easier."

"Shall we go?"

"Yes."

"The morgue is across the street, in the basement of the new jail building. Just let me call them to tell them we're coming. It's not real nice there, and if they're ready then we won't have to stay long."

Adele nodded, thinking that life was happening too fast at the moment. While Proffitt made his call, all she could think about was her shopping list.

When he returned Proffitt took her arm.

The morgue was smaller than Adele expected it to be. A red-cheeked and smiling young man named Eric came to them as they entered and asked, "Detective Proffitt?"

"That's right."

"I've got him ready for you."

Eric led the way to a hospitallike room. A long drawer with a body under a sheet stuck out from a wall of what looked like bus station lockers.

"They're doing the autopsy this afternoon," Eric said.

Proffitt guided Adele to the head end and nodded to Eric. Eric pulled the sheet back, exposing the dead man down to his chest.

Adele shook her head once, almost a twitch. She shook it again.

"Are you all right, ma'am?"

"It's *not* him," Adele said. "It's *not* him."

"I thought it wasn't," Proffitt said.

Adele's breathing stuttered.

Proffitt took her arm again and said, "Let's go."

11

As Proffitt walked back toward police headquarters Adele turned to him and said, "You knew, didn't you? It was more than just suspecting, wasn't it?"

"Well, yes."

"I don't understand."

"Detective Diehl went to the address on the ID in the wallet this morning. The woman living there said her husband went out last night after he got a phone call, about ten o'clock. He didn't come home. By this morning, when Diehl talked to her, she was pretty upset. The husband was not exactly a steady kind of fella, but he didn't usually just cut out like that. She thought he'd had an accident. Her husband's name was Brian Wampler."

"You mean—"

"Same name. Different man."

"But the note?"

"Diehl doesn't have any idea about that. The woman's husband was a beer distributor. His wife didn't know anything about social workers or what the note could mean."

Adele frowned and shook her head as she thought

about this. "Detective Proffitt, why did you bring me down here?"

"First, to make completely sure the dead man isn't the Brian Wampler you know."

"But your Detective Diehl must have brought the wife down to make a positive identification."

"Yes. But he could have had two jobs."

"No social worker would have the time to lead a double life as a beer distributor." Her tone was sarcastic, critical.

Proffitt shrugged unrepentantly. "It seemed a funny name for there to be two of them."

"That may well be," Adele said.

"Though if you look in the phone book, you'll find more than fifty Wamplers and lots of repeated first names."

Adele said nothing.

"But only the one *Brian*," Proffitt said. "And no other *B*."

Patiently Adele said, "Our Brian Wampler's phone number isn't in the book."

"I see."

"A lot of social workers have unlisted phones. Now he's married, you'd find our Brian Wampler's number under his wife's name. But it's probably not in the book yet. They haven't been married long."

"What's the wife's name?"

"Denise."

Proffitt made a note. Then he said, "Ma'am, it's a hell of a coincidence that some guy breaks into your office and then only a few hours later a man with the same name as someone who used to work for you gets murdered and left with a note about social workers on it."

"It does seem unlikely."

"If there's no connection, I'll be buttered for a snap bean."

"So are you saying that this man was killed because he

had the same name as the Brian Wampler who worked for us?"

"Your intruder copied a file. Could have been to get a social worker's name. It's just about the only way I can think of to line up the note and the dead man and your break-in."

They were silent for a moment before Proffitt continued, "Of course, Diehl is going into the dead Wampler's life and connections. Could be he'll come up with some other information that makes what I been thinking seem stupid."

Adele looked at the man. "But you've told Diehl what you suspect about the link between my intruder and the murder?"

"Not as yet."

Proffitt met her eyes and held the gaze. They stopped walking. "I needed you to see the body first. But I will talk to Diehl as soon as I leave you and see if he's interested."

Proffitt took a step, but when he realized Adele was not moving, he turned to face her. "What's the matter, ma'am?"

"It crossed my mind that maybe you plan to tell Detective Diehl about the connection to my break-in in such a vague way that he *won't* be interested."

"Now why would I do that?"

"You might do that because you think it's a good lead that only you should know about."

Proffitt's expression didn't change. He didn't speak.

"If you were to follow it up yourself, and it did turn out to be the right connection, you'd get a lot of credit, wouldn't you?"

Proffitt said evenly, "It would do me a powerful lot of good, ma'am."

"I see."

"A new boy—even one with a track record where he

comes from—has to prove himself all over in a big city department like this."

"I think you are an ambitious man, Detective Proffitt."

"We all set ourselves goals."

"I think I understand now why you were willing to spend a lot of time on my insignificant break-in this morning. You already knew about the body on the Circle, didn't you?"

"I knew there was another case to do with social workers."

Adele *tsk*ed.

"There are worse things for a policeman than ambition, ma'am."

"No doubt."

"Ma'am, back where I come from I was considered to be a pretty subtle fella, but you seem to see through me without even putting on your glasses."

"I'm not exactly criticizing you, Detective Proffitt. But I certainly prefer people to deal straight with me."

"I'll try to remember that."

"I'm not stupid. I'm not insensitive. If I feel someone's intentions are constructive I can be helpful. Even loyal. I can deal with gray areas as well as those that are just black or white."

"I'll try to remember that, too, ma'am."

Adele thought for a moment. "What time was the body found?"

"Five fifty-five this morning."

"Nobody saw it being put there? Dumped from a car, or whatever?"

"Not yet."

"What was the note written on, and how was it attached to the body?"

"I don't know, ma'am," Proffitt said. "I'll find out. But there's something more important to do first."

"What's that?"

"I need to talk to the social worker Brian Wampler.'"

"Because?"

"Because," Proffitt said, "chances are *he* is in danger. When—if—the killer finds out he got the wrong man, he'll likely want to go for the right one. Assuming what I'm assuming is the correct thing to assume. Ma'am."

Adele was silent, thinking about Brian Wampler.

Proffitt looked at his note. "So the home number is under his wife's name, Denise. Does he have a number at work?"

"Brian works for a private adoption agency now," Adele said. "I have the address and phone number back at the office. I have his home address there, too."

"What I'd like is for you to go back to your office and phone me with them."

"All right. I'll do that," Adele said.

They began to walk again.

After several seconds Proffitt said, "This morning you said you were going to have a look through some files."

"I found three cases where the records seemed to have been disturbed."

"I thought you said last night's guy only took one file out."

"He did."

"So the other two files were just put back incorrectly by your people?"

"Or all three," Adele said. "No guarantee any of these is the case the break-in man looked at."

"No," Proffitt said, agreeing. Then, "Seems to me it would also be a good idea to go through that file drawer to see which cases involved your Mr. Wampler."

"All right. But I'll call you with the addresses first because I may have to go out on an urgent visit before I can look through all the records in the drawer."

"You were working on something urgent last night, weren't you, ma'am?"

"That's right. But not the same case."

"Sounds like you spend a lot of your time under pressure."

"It varies," Adele said, "but yes."

Proffitt hesitated, then said, "Do you have time to eat, ma'am?"

"What do you mean?"

"Before that subtle, direct and powerful brain beats me to where I'm going, what I want is to ask you to have dinner with me tonight."

"Are we talking about a further business meeting or are you proposing a social contact?"

"I want to get on with this case as fast as I can," he said, "but I would be less than honest if I didn't answer your question by saying both."

"I see."

"What I thought was maybe we could meet up as soon as you were free this evening, but after you'd been through the files."

Adele thought for a moment, then said, measuredly, "All right. I don't see why we can't 'meet up' this evening, Sergeant Proffitt."

"Even people who aren't all that good friends call me Homer, ma'am."

"I'll try to remember."

"Thank you."

"But Homer, I will want to get home early."

"That suits me fine. Shall I fetch you from where you live or would you rather meet me?"

"I'll meet you."

"I'm kind of partial to Chinese food."

"All right."

"Do you know the Jade Garden?"

"That's quite close to my office."

He smiled. "In case you're having to work late again," he said.

"Barring some emergency, I'll be there by seven or a little after," Adele said.

"So will I."

"But if there's a problem, I'll call."

"That's fine."

"But let's get one thing clear, Homer. I pay for myself."

"You can pay for me, too, ma'am, if you really want to."

12

When Adele walked in the door of Hendricks Agency, the first person she saw was Brian Wampler.

Wampler, over six feet tall with light brown hair and a big, ingratiating smile, was sitting on the edge of Martin's desk.

Martin looked uncomfortable, straining to be polite.

As Adele proceeded into the room, Patrick whispered to her, "Brian's here."

"The fair Adele!" Wampler said as he caught sight of her. Tina McLarnon stood near her desk, holding a cup of coffee. Anna Pike was not in the office.

"Brian," Adele said. "How nice to see you."

"Living, breathing and fighting fit." He jumped up into a brief combination of dancing and shadowboxing.

"How do you happen to be here?"

"Martin was kind enough to make a condolence call to Denise. It would have been quite a shock for the poor girl if I hadn't been sitting across the room from her."

"We all talked about it," Martin said defensively. "We agreed someone should phone Denise. It wasn't that we were going to tell her. It was a matter of sounding her out and asking, maybe, if she knew where Brian was."

Patrick nodded, confirming the statement.

Adele said, "Uh huh."

"As things were, it was rather embarrassing for our poor Martin," Wampler said.

He nodded to Martin. As he did so Adele saw that Tina was struggling with her emotions. It was the first time that Wampler had returned to the office since he left his job there.

He said, "I thought I'd come over to make it clear that the stories of my demise are definitely premature."

"We certainly were all worried," Adele said. "And, of course, equally pleased and relieved that our fears were groundless."

"I am moved by your collective concern," Wampler said.

"As you're here," Adele said, "do you think I could have a word with you?"

"Sure, sweetie. In your office?"

"Please. Go on in. I'll be with you in a moment."

"Just like old times." Wampler walked easily into Adele's office.

To Tina, Adele said, "Are you all right?"

Tina nodded, didn't speak and wasn't convincing.

Martin said, "It's all been pretty upsetting. For everyone, one way and another. Tina was . . . I think it's fair to say Tina was very upset when she got back and heard the news. That's when I called Denise."

Adele nodded.

"I'm all right," Tina said. "Really. It wasn't just this. I had a difficult session this afternoon."

"That was with young Clyde?" Adele asked.

"Yes. And it went badly."

Adele frowned. "How do you mean?"

"I met Brenda beforehand and we talked about what sort of situation and what sort of child we were expecting."

Adele nodded.

"But when we went to the house to interview the child, it was not at all what we had anticipated. This boy is small and doesn't even look physically capable. He's also quiet and shy."

"How do things stand then?"

"Brenda is arranging medical examinations for the three girls and the boy. The girls' mothers think we're all crazy. And Clyde's mother went absolutely bananas about Granny and says the old woman's got sex on the brain and doesn't have a clue what she's talking about. The situation just doesn't feel like one where anybody's in danger, you know what I mean?"

Adele nodded.

"On the other hand, talking to Granny again alone, she was adamant about what she saw. And everyone admits that the children play together in the garage. So for the time being we continue to take it seriously."

"Sounds complicated."

"Brenda will be back in touch when the medicals are arranged. I'll go out again to help her."

Adele nodded. "All right," she said. "Keep me informed."

"Of course."

Adele turned to Patrick. "What is Anna up to?"

"Anna said that she had to see Jaimie Norton and that she had another stop as well," Patrick said. "She might not get back again this afternoon."

Brian Wampler sat as easily on the edge of Adele's desk as he had on Martin's. He said, "Nice to see that you are as smoldering and erotic and gorgeous as ever."

"Things going well with your adoption people?"

"The adoption business is booming," Brian said. He fingered the fabric of his shirt. "I always said that my skin was made for silk."

"That's not silk."

"It soon will be."

Adele raised her eyebrows. "I've just come from a policeman who wants to talk to you," she said.

"Being at home in the afternoon isn't a criminal offense yet, is it?" Wampler said.

"You don't work for me anymore, Brian."

"But despite myself I still respond to those standards of exhausting overwork and hyperresponsibility that you set so impressively."

"I *was* relieved to find out that the dead man wasn't you after all," Adele said.

"Perhaps the shock has made you aware of my charms at last."

"You'll never know."

"I live in perpetual hope."

"The policeman thinks that you may be in danger."

Wampler smiled more broadly. When he saw that Adele didn't appear to be joking, his face dropped its grin. "Are you serious?"

"Sure," Adele said.

"Explain."

"This detective thinks that whoever killed the other Brian Wampler meant to kill you."

"Kill? Me?"

"Yes."

"That's ridiculous. Why would anybody want to kill me?"

"I'm only passing on what the policeman said to me. Why don't you talk to him and let him explain."

"I'll do that," Wampler said. He considered. "Shit!"

"I'll call him for you now," Adele said. She began to dial.

13

WHILE Brian Wampler talked to Proffitt on the telephone, Adele left the office to follow up King Smith's information about Donna East. And her children.

Although the address Smith had given was not far away, Adele drove, and then cruised slowly along the street until she found what turned out to be a house built in the 1920's as a luxury home for a large family.

The luxury was long departed. The three-story brick building had been divided into apartments. The yard was a mess. Gang and obscene graffitti on the front wall were gray and old.

Of the eight bells by the front door, only two sported legible names. Smith's was one, claiming apartment 3A in a hand that was as flowery and controlled as, in appearance, he himself was not. The other was for "Basement" and the name "Armes" was written in pencil. Stuck sideways into one of the unlabeled bell mountings, a piece of cardboard bore the word "Vacancies."

Adele did not ring Smith's bell. The front door was clearly ajar. She entered.

The entrance hallway smelled of urine. At the bottom

of the stairs that led to upper floors there was an orange peel cupped around some coffee grounds.

The dark walls were multicolored, but only one of the decorative ingredients was paint.

The edges of the stairs showed a carpet either side of stringy remains in the middles.

Was it "abuse" to keep children inside an apartment when what was outside was like this?

Adele climbed carefully to the top, watching each foot-fall. Many of the stairs seemed to squeal under her weight.

As she approached the third-floor landing, she heard human noises.

They were muted and unclear at first, but by the time Adele stepped out of the stairwell the sound was recognizable as the urgent, breathy moan of a woman in orgasm.

It went on and on and came from behind the door marked 3A.

Adele turned to the other door on the landing, the one that had to have been Donna East's.

There was a bell button, and Adele pushed it twice, although she couldn't hear whether it had rung inside or not.

After a pause, she tried the knob. The door gave way and opened. She entered, closed it behind her and called, "Miss East? Miss East?"

There was no response.

Adele found herself in a kind of all-purpose living room. There was a small television set, a couch, a folded bed, a kitchen table and chairs.

Everything was stunningly clean, and the room's lack of odor was a positive relief.

She moved around the room. Two chests of drawers were topped by a few children's coloring books. On the television was a framed photograph of two young girls hugging each other and laughing. They were dressed identically and had the distinguishing facial features of mild Down's syndrome.

The two windows overlooked an alley.

There was a closed internal door. Adele opened it.

On the other side she found a narrow kitchen with rope crisscrossed around the ceiling like vaulting. The rope was studded with clothespins, though no clothing hung from it. A single wooden chair seemed the only access to the clotheslines.

Two plastic bowls stood in one another on the work surface by the single sink. There were cupboards, drawers, an electric stove, a refrigerator, an iron. A pull-down ironing board was built into one end of the room. There was no washing machine.

There were three more doors.

One went outside, leading to a back porch.

The second opened to a toilet. No bathtub or shower.

The third had a large bolt across it so that it could be securely closed. When Adele slid the bolt open and pulled on the door, she found what must originally have been a broom closet or a pantry. Now the closet was filled with two large shelves, each extending the full length and width of the space.

Both shelves were made up as beds.

A vision of the two laughing little girls bolted for the night into an airless closet burst into Adele's mind and was profoundly disquieting.

She sat on the chair, and thought hard and breathed heavily. She felt strongly that whatever had happened in this empty space had been utterly, seriously *wrong*.

She felt a sudden passionate *need* to know what had happened to Donna East. And the two little girls.

This wave of passion, the involvement, was something she had not felt for a long time. It was followed by memories of an awful time of her own, when she was a young woman alone with a daughter. Fleeing in a panic to escape the girl's father. Sleeping two nights in a car. Pressured by her own parents to go back to him, denied their aid because she was "being foolish and hysterical." When she knew it was *wrong* to give in.

This was the man who had called to be the first to wish Lucy a happy Valentine's Day. If Lucy *knew* what the creature was capable of when he had the control, the power, over another person's life . . .

Or thought he had.

Night flight, it had been. With baby. With the seeping wounds that come from the intimate war of two supposedly intelligent people who don't hit each other. When only one of the combatants is whole and human.

Well, humane.

The twenty-year-old hatred lived again for many, many seconds.

Finally Adele shook her head to clear it of history.

Jesus! It had been years since all that had swept over her.

Some people quiver in the night from their mortality . . .

She stood up. Shook her head again and looked around the kitchen. She saw, on the wall, patches of a previous color showing through the paint. It was as if repeated washings, scrubbings, had worn away the top coat.

Vision of the mother scrubbing, the children whimpering behind the bolted door.

A kind of prison—prison beds for children living with an imprisoned mother.

Adele went out the back door.

She stepped onto a porch that was almost another world. About nine feet square, the porch was roofless. In each corner and in the middle of each side a wooden pillar stood well above her head. Pillar to pillar all around the porch were shelves. But each of the porch shelves supported a plant box, and each of these was filled with the soil and the dead stalks of a fertile summer's growth of leaves and flowers. Each pair of pillars shared five shelves, five troughs. The effect was to make the porch a kind of room of the outdoors.

Somehow it was like stepping into the country, and despite the season the porch was as much a place of life as the apartment was of a kind of death.

A stool and a watering can stood in a corner. Next to them was a weather-beaten wooden rocking chair.

A fierce wind rocked only the dead vegetation.

Adele returned to the kitchen.

She needed to be busy.

Methodically she began to examine every closed space in the apartment.

The kitchen cupboards were stocked with convenience foods. There were no implements for any kind of more complicated cooking.

She found cutlery and plates for four. Four glasses, four cups. Four Deputy Dawg placemats.

The Monday visitor stayed for a meal?

There were a lot of washing and cleaning articles beneath the sink. And an array of fertilizers, pesticides and fungicides.

In the living room drawers Adele found only a few items of clothing, but as King Smith's description of Donna East's life had suggested, they all bore mail-order company labels.

Adele emptied each drawer, examined each item. After finishing one drawer she repacked it and started on the next.

What clothes were left were in good condition. Nothing old or frayed. She found no children's toys, nothing cuddly or personal. That was almost reassuring. Maybe such things had been taken with them.

In one drawer, at the bottom, were a dozen mail-order catalogs. Beneath them order forms.

And a single anomalous item. It was a business card. For a "Clint Honneker" who was "an official pollster" for "Hoosier Opinion Research Systems." The company name was unfamiliar.

The card bore no address or telephone number. It was creased, as if it had been carried for a long time before being put in the bottom of the drawer to be flattened, preserved, by the catalogs.

In another drawer Adele found two bottles of simple medicine: children's aspirin and, half empty, cough syrup.

Suddenly, with no warning, a voice behind her cracked into her consciousness: "What do you think you're doing?"

She nearly fell as she whirled to face the sound.

King Smith, with a flannel shirt unbuttoned over a "Kill a baby seal today!" T-shirt, stood inside the front door, leaning on his cane, grinning. "I thought I caught somebody coming up the stairs," he said.

"I'm surprised you could hear anything at all," Adele said, catching her breath.

Smith looked smug. "Hot stuff, that Anna bitch from your office. She sure knows what she likes."

Adele said nothing.

Smith, pushing childishly for a response said, "Quite an apology. Are all you social workers like that?"

Adele said, "Mr. Smith, have you heard any more of Donna East or her children?"

He shrugged, then answered the question. "No."

"Do you have any idea whatever of how to get in touch with anybody who might know something about them?"

Smith's expression suggested that he was beginning to catch on that Adele was talking about something serious. He shook his head.

"Did Donna East ever say anything about where she had grown up?"

"She referred to herself once as a Hoosier."

"Born in Indiana?"

"Presumably. But she didn't say where."

"You said earlier that she had talked to you for a long time. There must be a number of things that she said that you didn't tell me."

"Oh, sure, but not facts. She didn't talk a lot about facts."

"Nothing about this 'lawyer'?"

"No. Look, Miss . . . Thing . . ."

"What?" Adele asked.

"I don't know if it will help . . ."

"What?"

"I'm a playwright."

"So you said."

"A lot of times when I have encounters with people, afterward I write it down."

Adele was unsure what he meant.

"I told you before my recall for conversation is good. What it is, is there's something in my brain that if I get writing pretty soon after it's taken place, I can almost *hear* what was said again. It might not be exactly word for word—I've never tested it against a tape—but I'd bet it was right. Or just about right, I'm sure of that."

"And you wrote something like that after your conversation with Donna on Tuesday night."

"Yes."

"May I have it?"

"Certainly not! Not 'have' it."

"But can I make a copy? Will you let me do that?"

He shrugged.

"Let's do that now. I've got a copy machine in my office."

Smith was hesitant.

"Is there a problem?"

"Can I wait outside while you photocopy it?"

"All right."

"It's just I've got all this thing with your tough little Anna bitch in my head now. I don't want to see her again before I can get all *that* down on paper."

14

King Smith twitched outside the Hendricks office until Adele brought his eleven pencil-covered yellow legal pad pages out and handed them back.

"You took your time," he said pettishly.

"I had to experiment to find the right settings for the photocopier."

"I got very edgy waiting out here," Smith said, sounding almost pathetic. In a backward way it was an apology. "I don't normally let anybody see anything that's in a draft form."

"You're making a play out of this?"

"I may," he said. "I'm not really all that good at making things up, so I use things that I hear." He opened his eyes wide for a moment. "That's one of the reasons I am sometimes needlessly abrasive."

"Oh yes?"

"If I can *cause* unusual conversations . . . stimulate people I encounter to find words other than their routine 'please' and 'thank you's . . .'"

"So you work at being unpleasant?" she said. Thinking, It can't make you crack a sweat, that particular kind of "work."

"I don't think *unpleasant*," King Smith said. "More *provocative*."

"I see."

"Of course sometimes things just happen to me. Like Donna coming across the landing after being neighbors all those months. But other times, I 'seed' the situation. I grow things to hear. People performing their characters for me."

"Oh."

"I think of each conversation as a fragment. The one with Donna. The ones with your Anna that I will be doing in a few minutes. Eventually, when I get fragments that fit with each other, I put them together. It's like making a pot out of shards."

"Oh," Adele said.

"Do you know much about the writer's mind?"

"No."

"I thought not," he said. His attention seemed to drift away. He shifted position, leaned more heavily on his Shakespeare cane and snapped his head, first to the right and then to the left. He had clearly become uncomfortable.

"Anna is not in the office," Adele said.

"She said she had a lot to do this afternoon."

"She certainly does."

"But she might come back."

"That wouldn't be a problem for you, would it?"

"As it stands . . . At the moment . . ." He made oval gestures with his hands. "There is a voluptuousness to our encounters. The words to describe it, the words that were spoken, they are all very sharp in my mind."

"Oh."

"But if I talk about it, everything will blur."

"Do you want me to drive you back home? I promise I won't say a thing."

"No. The walk will help me shake you off. It'll get me back in the groove of what I want to write about."

"Have any of your plays ever been produced, Mr. Smith?"

"Of course," he said. Stiffly he turned and walked away.

Adele telephoned Carollee Fleetwood and explained what she had found at Donna East's apartment.

"I don't like the sound of those beds in the closet," Fleetwood said. "Weren't there air holes in the door or anything?"

"No," Adele said. Then she explained about King Smith's "fragment" from his conversation with Donna East.

"I haven't read his notes carefully yet, but they do seem to follow what he told me before. But I did look up the name on the business card, Clint Honneker, in the telephone directory. There is no Clint Honneker listed. Or any other kind of Honneker. Or a Hoosier Opinion Research Systems."

"Are you suggesting that you think the business card is a fake?"

"I suppose. I certainly don't like it not having an address or phone number on it." Adele mused for a moment about what the purpose of a fake opinion poll business card might be.

"Still, best to try Information. It could conceivably be a new number."

"All right," Adele said. Though the card looked old.

Fleetwood was silent for a moment before she said, "What you've got is more a suspicious disappearance than just a missing persons case, Adele. I probably ought to pass it over to our Detective division."

"I met one of your detectives today, about another case. I don't know whether you'll know him. A Homer Proffitt."

"Ah, Proffitt," Fleetwood said.

"You do know him?"

"Only by reputation. He was some kind of golden boy in Evansville who quit to come up here. I don't know what the story is, but he's considered a comer."

"He certainly struck me as hungry to make his mark."

"It's hard, you know, for officers who transfer. They may have a lot of experience and background, but they still have to go through our training and probationary period just like anybody else. People I know say he's supposed to be very good. Apparently there was some case in Evansville that he cracked—three poisoning murders that had been open for ten years."

"To my untutored ear that sounds pretty impressive."

"It certainly isn't the kind of thing that happens every day," Fleetwood said.

"Might a 'suspicious disappearance' not be grand enough for him to work on?"

"I don't know what kind of workload he's got. Do you want me to ask him to take it on?"

"It would be simpler for me to work with one person, rather than two."

"I'll give him a call," Fleetwood said. Then, "They also say he's rather interesting-looking. Kind of small and intense. I'll be quite happy for the excuse to make his acquaintance."

"Thank you," Adele said, wondering why she hadn't said she was meeting the man for dinner.

Fleetwood said, "I'll also run 'Donna East' through our computers and some of the data banks we're hooked up to. You don't know the names of her children, do you?"

"No."

"I can but try. And I'll run 'Clint Honneker' and 'Hoosier Opinion Research Systems' through. We might have some references, somewhere, only a microchip away."

"Anything you feel able to do," Adele said with gratitude.

Finally, at five o'clock, Adele got back to the three A TO H files she had pulled in the morning.

The cases seemed to have nothing in common except

their out-of-order pages. One involved a six-year-old boy who had been taken into care after physical attacks by his violent stepfather. Another was a case of sexual abuse of an eight-year-old girl by her grandfather. The third had to do with a disabled single woman who had decided to live in an apartment on her own.

Only the third case had been Brian Wampler's before he changed jobs.

Adele read the file notes carefully, looking for ways to criticize their social work content. Trying to see what the violent visitor so hostile to social workers might have been thinking about.

She didn't find anything that "felt" the right kind of thing. But then there was no guarantee any of these cases was the one the intruder had copied.

She closed the files on her desk.

She looked at the photocopy of King Smith's "fragment."

She thought about going back to the A TO H drawer to pull all the other cases involving Brian Wampler.

And were there other things she should be doing?

She went to the A TO H drawer.

She opened it.

She realized that she just didn't want to go through the files now.

It took her a moment to realize why.

She didn't want to be left alone in the office.

So instead she locked up and went home to try to convince Lucy to do the shopping while she took a bath and got ready to go out for dinner.

15

"MOST old windows are easy enough to open from the outside," Proffitt said.

He rummaged through his jacket pockets until he found and withdrew a rectangle of stiff blue plastic. He passed it across the table. "I got that from a thief down where I used to live. I can get through a lot of doors and most old windows with that and a little bit of . . ." From his wallet he took a looped piece of wire.

"Nice company you keep," Adele said. "Or is that what they teach you in police school?"

"Mostly they try to teach us how to keep our tempers when we're being called bad names and what the law says and how to kill people before they kill us and how to keep a lid on what we say to the press."

"Oh."

"Sensitivity training. It's very big these days."

Adele thought she saw a bit of self-mockery in his expression that she hadn't heard in his voice. But she wasn't sure enough to react to it.

Oh, the agonies of first dates . . . Hmmm, I suppose he is interesting-looking, if you think positively.

Proffitt was saying, "In fact, it's a detailed training program they have here. And a damn sight better than the first one I went on. What problems they get are a whole lot more likely to come from the material that goes through the program than from the program itself."

"It wasn't a very serious question, Homer."

"No, ma'am, but I'm a whole lot better with serious answers than with your banter kind of talk."

Adele tilted her head. "And now I think you're joking with me."

"You city girls sure are hard to please." He turned to his plate.

Adele said, "Did Carollee Fleetwood catch you this afternoon?"

"The sergeant from Missing Persons?"

"That's right."

He smiled. "She told me about a puzzling disappearance and asked if I'd look into it."

"And what did you say?"

"I said that I would be honored and proud to see whether there was anything I could find out."

Adele chuckled. "I bet you did, too."

"Yes, ma'am."

"Yes, ma'am," Adele mimicked.

"It'll take you a whole lot of practice to get that sounding really right," Proffitt said.

"Carollee explained the details of the case then?"

"A woman and her two little girls gone from their apartment. A business card and some pills and some clothes and not a lot else left behind."

"I think the card is a fake," Adele said. "There's no listing in the telephone book and nothing with Information."

"Could be an old card. A business gone bust."

"I didn't think of that."

"I can find out tomorrow."

"How?"

"Call another opinion poll company. They'll know about their opposition."

"Sounds good," she said. Adele found the card in her handbag and passed it across the table. "You might as well keep it."

"OK."

"I did remember something else while I was in the bathtub," Adele said.

"What was that?"

"The man who visited Donna East supposedly told Welfare that he was supporting her. Whether he actually did or not, it seems possible that MCDPW has records on Donna. And maybe the children."

"MCDPW, ma'am?"

"Sorry. Marion County Department of Public Welfare. I can check with them in the morning."

"Sounds good," Proffitt said. "With a reasonable run of the dice we ought to be able to get a little somewhere."

Adele nodded approval. Then asked, "The dice? Are you a gambling man, Homer?"

"Everybody is, one way or another, ma'am. But I was referring more to life's dice than any other kind."

"And what kind of gambling do you go in for?"

"Danger gives me a buzz. Ma'am."

"Are you being serious now, or are you playing with me again?"

"Ma'am, I'd have thought that 'playing' with you might be just a little *too* dangerous."

Adele breathed out heavily. "I don't know what to make of you, Proffitt."

"And here I always figure that I'm real straightforward and easy to please."

She looked at him.

He looked at her.

She said, "Let's talk about the Brian Wampler case."

"Your Brian Wampler struck me as a bit of a slippery customer," Proffitt said.

"Did you actually meet him or just talk on the phone?"

"I asked him to come in for a chat."

"And did he?"

"He did. But it was as if there was always extra stuff going on behind what he was talking about."

Adele said, "I feel that he's one of those people who is insecure inside and so he has to be devious and have secrets in his private life so he can feel in charge of something."

"What's he like as a social worker?"

"He's intelligent, quick about a lot of things. Generally he's pretty good."

Proffitt chuckled and shook his head at her. "Is it a law with you folks that you got to say the five percent good before you can launch into the ninety-five percent bad?"

"It's not like that," Adele said, but with her expression she acknowledged that she had been caught trying hard to be "fair." "But I don't like him. You're right."

"Tell me why you don't like him."

"He got romantically involved with a couple of women in the office when he worked for me, and he treated them badly."

"Is he one of those guys that's got to make a pass at every lady he meets?" Proffitt asked.

"I think his 'charm' problem goes deeper than that," Adele said. "As a social worker he is much too inclined to try to sweet-talk clients instead of doing the routine work necessary to establish a practical relationship with them."

"That would be primarily women?"

"Yes. Most of the adults we deal with are women. Now his kind of style is all right for certain kinds of problems and it might well get a client smiling, but it's not the all-purpose basis of a social work relationship that Brian thinks it is."

"You've talked to him about it?"

"His brain understands what I say. But I don't think he can control himself."

"Did you fire him, ma'am?"

"It might have come to that. A case he was in charge of blew up and he made a mess of it. A single mother tried to commit suicide because of things she thought he had promised her. About whether she would be allowed to keep her baby or not."

"She didn't die?"

"She made a vegetable out of herself."

"Was it Wampler's fault?"

"He covered himself technically. But the kind of thing she claimed he said to her sounded—to me—very much like what he might well have said."

"What happened?"

"He quit and went to another job. The head of the agency insisted that it be dropped at that point, and it was."

"Another social work job?"

"Not really. He's with a private adoption agency now." Adele shrugged. "It wasn't a very happy set of circumstances."

"Well," Proffitt said, "that's all very interesting." He raised his eyes and blinked a few times.

Adele said, "What did you say to Brian?"

"I told him I think he's in danger of being murdered."

"Good heavens. How did he take that?"

"I think it's fair to say he didn't quite know what to make of it. I also asked him to think about the cases he had when he worked for you. Whether any of them involved people who were so aggrieved they might want him dead. He couldn't think of any offhand."

"You think it was my intruder, don't you?"

"My hypothesis is that your man last night got the name Brian Wampler from your files, looked in the telephone book, and killed the only Brian Wampler he found there."

Adele was silent for a moment.

"And I'll tell you this, ma'am. If I'm right, you sure were in the presence of one dangerous dude. We're talking premeditated murder. And we're talking about a man who will do it all again if—when—he finds out that he got the wrong guy. You think about that."

"I'd rather not," Adele said, trying to be light.

"I *could* be wrong," Proffitt said. "Could be something else happening altogether. But Diehl hasn't found anything in the dead guy's life that looks like it'll provide a different answer."

"If you're right," Adele said, "shouldn't something be done?"

"I warned Mr. Wampler. He agreed to be careful."

"Did he take it seriously?"

"I'm not sure I could tell what he took to heart and what he didn't."

Adele nodded.

"Diehl wasn't ready to assign officers to guarding him. And I think that may be fair enough. I do feel we have a little time before the intruder finds he got the wrong man. And the guy could well have left town anyway, thinking his job was done."

"You think he lives elsewhere?"

"He hasn't got his face in our picture files," Proffitt said. "And he has to break into your office to get a social worker's name on a case he's so upset about. So it sounds like he doesn't have good sources of information here."

"So, what are you going to do next about Brian?"

"I'll talk to him again tomorrow in case he's remembered anything. But I would like to have a little more that I can ask him about."

"Like what?"

Proffitt said, "You're going to tell me now that those three files you examined didn't make any reference to Wampler."

"Well, as a matter of fact, one did."

"What kind of case was it?"

"Back-up support for a woman who was a Thalidomide victim. Missing both legs and most of an arm. The agency has had her as a client for a long time, but now she's decided to try to live on her own."

"No family?"

"Parents wouldn't take her home from the hospital when she was born."

"Sounds sad."

"On paper. But she's quite a gal. She got some money in the settlement and she is very determined to be independent. It's a struggle. But the last I heard she was doing all right."

"I would like to talk to her," Proffitt said. It was stronger than a request.

"The case has gone to another social worker, Tina McLarnon. I'll ask her to set up an appointment."

"Like tomorrow morning?"

Adele nodded.

"Ma'am."

"What?"

"There's something else I have to tell you."

"What's that?"

"The coroner says that the dead Brian Wampler had his neck *and* back broken."

Adele was silent.

"Our guys think it just about had to be done by somebody who was real strong."

"I see," she said.

"Which could be a real big man."

Adele was silent.

"So I think you've got to be warned too, ma'am."

"What are you saying, Homer?"

"If your intruder was the killer, then you're the only person we've got who has seen him and who could identify him."

16

"A business dinner, eh?" Al said on the telephone. "With a handsome young policeman."

"So handsome! So young!" Adele said.

"What, may I ask, might his marital status be?"

"I don't know, now that you mention it."

"Doesn't even care, the brazen hussy."

'Mmmm, so *young!* I had *such* a good time that I just *had* to call and tell you about it."

Turning away from the light tone of the conversation Al said, "I've got no claims on you. You know that."

Adele laughed because she had managed to extract a serious reaction from him.

"All right, all right!" he said, annoyed.

She laughed again.

"Nervous giggles," Al said, "because you feel guilty about having frisky meals while I'm slaving on your daughter's rich boyfriend all hours."

"Really?" Adele said. "Have you found anything out about this Fritz person?"

"I see I have your attention again," Al said. "The old fella's not such a bad deal when he's out doing the background work that's too tasteless for you even to admit you want done, eh?"

But he didn't push the game and continued, "I talked to the professor who is supervising Fritz Kory Goodhew's masters thesis. Our Fritz is an ambitious, not particularly imaginative young man who is especially interested in the ways sociology can be applied to business decisions. His thesis will be based on an analysis of a technically sophisticated consumer questionnaire that is really measuring the reliability of the responses given rather than the content. That's a quote, but don't ask me which bit."

"Sounds fascinating," Adele said.

"At this stage Fritz is spending a lot of time going door-to-door with this questionnaire."

"It seems to be my day for opinion pollers."

"I think," Al said, "that he has harnessed Lucy to help him."

"How?"

"To go with him so he can quantify the 'response reliability factor for couples on the doorstep compared to individuals.' According to this professor."

"That's what they're up to each night, is it?"

"Not disappointed, are you?"

"I don't know," Adele said.

"I didn't have a long time with this professor guy—in my guise as a personnel recruitment legman. I'm on two cases at the moment. Neither is interesting, but at least my paying clients don't tease me."

"I am grateful," Adele said. "Stupid as I feel hearing about Fritz from you instead of Lucy."

"Your interest is more than understandable, even if involving me feels murky."

"She's been so *funny* recently. Moody."

"I wish I could help, but I hardly qualify as an expert on girls."

"Poor Albert."

"I stopped in at my mother's luncheonette today."

"How is she?"

"All things considered, pretty good. Except she's got a seventeen-year-old juvenile delinquent living in there now."

"Living in?"

"Yeah. She claims she's training him to be a short-order cook."

"You sound doubtful."

"He didn't strike me as the hash-slinger type. But hell, what do I know about kids these days?"

"You think he's taking advantage of her somehow?"

"I'm worried he's going to steal everything that isn't bolted to the floor, but I'll reserve judgment."

Adele considered for a moment and then said, "Let's go there for lunch sometime soon."

"That would be nice. I'd be grateful for your professional opinion."

"Can't be tomorrow, Al. All this police stuff, on top of our regular work—things are frantic."

"Sometime when you're not quite so busy with young handsome policemen then." He mused and said, "So, what wisdom did you receive from your fortune cookie?"

"'He who has imagination without learning has wings but no feet.'"

"Sounds all right if all you want is to keep flying. And what was your policeman's fortune then?"

"He opened his cookie and there was nothing inside."

"Didn't he ask for another one?"

"No. He took it as a deep message in itself."

"A philosophical cop—my God."

"He *is* different from most of the other police I know."

"Young, handsome . . ."

Adele's voice abruptly took on a serious tone. "Albert," she said, "the real reason I called . . ."

Instantly serious in response, "Tell me."

"This cop thinks *I'm* in danger. Real, physical danger."

"I suppose I should have guessed *you'd* be here on Valentine's Day morning," Lucy said.

"All heart, that's me," Al said.

"If I'd known I would have bought the mandatory gallon of orange juice when *I* went shopping all *alone* yesterday evening."

"We didn't know that I'd be staying over," Albert said.

"You mad, impulsive things," Lucy said.

"Would you believe that I came as your mother's bodyguard?"

Lucy made a sour-taste face.

Al laughed at his unintentional double meaning.

"So," Lucy said, "didn't Mom get what she wanted from her policeman date?" Then, with transparent artifice: "Have I made a terrible 'oopsie' by mentioning it?"

"You better ask her, honey."

"I'm not a 'honey,'"

"I'm putting extra sugary words into what I'm saying to mask my annoyance at your being so pesty."

"Don't mind *me*," Lucy said. "I'm only the only daughter."

"I know all about daughters," Al said. "I've got one of my own."

"How is Sam these days?" Lucy asked.

"She's all right. The last letter I got she was living with an American sculptor somewhere in southern France."

"Don't you mind that?"

"I like sculpture."

"That's *not* what I mean."

"It's not for a distant father to approve or disapprove. I'm just grateful the wench still writes to me."

"She's out of college then?"

"Last spring."

"Did you go to her graduation?"

"She didn't graduate."

"Oh."

"It's a long story. But she hasn't told it to me yet."

"How long has it been since you saw her?"

"Years," Al said. He began to count on his fingers.

"Don't you miss seeing her?"

"I've been missing seeing her ever since her mother decamped to Switzerland."

"Why don't you go visit her?"

Al considered this.

"Do it," Lucy said.

"Yeah, I think I just might."

Lucy paused. "I'm sorry for being mean to you."

"It's not a problem, kid."

"I'm just feeling kind of . . . kind of dispossessed."

"It's all part of the fledging."

"I wish I were as easygoing as you are."

"I wish I were as easygoing as I am, too."

"Mother seems to be so much busier these days."

"I think," Al said, "that you may just be noticing it more."

"I suppose," Lucy said. Then, "I *am* sorry when I'm 'pesty.' But I don't seem to be able to help being irritable."

"You got anything special on your mind?"

"Not really."

Albert waited.

"Well . . ."

"What sort of thing is worrying you?"

Lucy leaned forward. "Al, do you think Mother would be furious if I moved out?"

"You mean in with someone or just out?"

"Just out, at least for the time being."

Al considered. "I don't think she's really thought about it."

"Exactly!" Lucy said. "She acts as if I'm going to live here forever."

"I meant thought about it as a practical proposition. She knows full well that your days with her in this house are numbered."

"Well, I've been thinking about it, and I'm worried she'll go through the roof."

"It's always going to be harder when an only daughter has been brought up alone by her mother."

"I feel so guilty it makes me mad."

"Talk to her, kid."

"I wondered if maybe you would. It wouldn't seem so—so definitive if *you* raised the subject with her. If you do it right."

"You haven't, perhaps, got a script for me, have you?"

"I did make a few notes. You know, pros and cons. But they were more for me." She paused. "Do you want to see them?"

"No thanks."

"Oh."

"It'll come better from you, Lucy."

"I thought you might say that."

"Because it's true."

"Maybe."

They sat in silence for a few moments. Then Lucy tossed her head from side to side to feel the swish of her hair.

"You were such a sweet child," Al said.

"Take a hike, gumshoe."

"So, what have you got on today?" Al asked.

"It's classes, classes, classes all day long for me. Higher education in this country has become incredibly boring."

"You must get some social relief from your school-work occasionally."

"None. Even when I go out all we talk about is this thesis my friend is writing."

"Is that"—deciding to be ignorant—"the beloved Arthur?"

"Who? Oh, Arthur. Good God, I haven't been going out with Arthur for *ages*. It's beloved Fritz now. He's a real laugh. I thought Mom would have told you."

"We've been preoccupied with other things," Al said.

"I *bet* you have," Lucy said. "Disgusting!"

17

ADELE called Frances Tounley at MCPWD as soon as she got into the office.

There were a number of key people at Welfare, but their quality varied. The theory was that the comparatively low pay pushed the best people elsewhere. The effect was not nearly so dramatic among social workers as it was among the welfare department's lawyers, but it was real. Over the years Adele had found Tounley to be efficient, sympathetic and helpful. Adele tried to steer all the agency's contact with Welfare through her.

Tounley listened carefully as Adele explained what she knew about the Donna East case.

"You'll be wanting me to see whether Donna East ever came to our attention," she said.

"Exactly so," Adele said.

Tounley agreed to check the records for Donna East and call back.

After finishing the call, Adele was about to get up and come out of her office when Tina popped her head in through the doorway. "Got a minute?"

"Come in."

Tina entered, and glanced behind her. "I wanted to alert you to possible trouble."

"Oh yes?"

"Patrick gave Anna a huge valentine this morning. It was *this* big! And Anna just dropped it in the wastepaper basket. Patrick's awfully upset."

"I sometimes think Anna is very good for Patrick."

"What?"

"She'll help him grow up, fast," Adele said. "We've got a busy day, Tina. I was about to round everybody up for Friday meeting. Could you call them in for me?"

"Sure."

"Oh, and before you go, the policeman working on our break-in case would like to visit one of your clients today."

"One of mine?"

"Nora Harrington."

"What does he want to see Nora about?"

"He thinks she may have information that will be useful." Adele shrugged as if she had no idea about details. "Could you give her a call, warn her, and see what time would suit her?"

"Sure." Then Tina frowned. "Am I supposed to be there?"

"You're welcome. I may go along since it has to do with the break-in. But I don't see any reason for you to go, if you don't want to."

Tina shrugged. "I've got plenty else to do if there's no need for me."

A few minutes later all three agency social workers came to Adele's office for the end-of-week discussion of the handling of the new cases that had been referred to them, as well as a general update on how things stood with existing cases.

"Apart from police-type matters," Adele said, "it has been a comparatively quiet week—"

"In Lake Woebegon," Martin interrupted. "Sorry."

"For actual work," Adele said. "We've picked up some long-term referrals from Welfare, and there's a new case having to do with young children who seem to be sexually active. Also a possible disappearance of some children with their mother. Tina, perhaps you could outline what's happened with your Clyde."

"You may remember an old woman who came into the office yesterday," Tina McLarnon began.

Four routine referrals were discussed and assigned. Developments in other specific cases that were of general office interest were noted, social worker by social worker. Adele was always last in these rounds, and when she had finished, Martin Cretney asked, "Is there any more information about the killing yesterday?"

"Not a lot."

"It says in the *Star* this morning that the victim was a beer salesman. And that the police don't know of a reason for the reference to social workers on the note."

"It says that in the newspaper?" Adele asked. She was clearly surprised.

"Yes," Martin said.

There were murmurs of agreement.

Adele exhaled heavily. She frowned.

"And it was on the news this morning," Tina said.

"Is that important?" Anna asked.

Adele said, "I know that as of last night the police certainly weren't of any fixed mind about why the man was killed or about the meaning of the note."

"Oh," Martin said.

"However, one speculation is that the killer got the wrong man."

"You mean . . . ?" Martin asked.

"That he may have been after our Brian Wampler after all," Adele said.

"Oh!" Tina went pale.

"It's just a theory," Adele said. "But they *are* having trouble making sense of the note. Brian was warned about the possibility yesterday. Presumably if this kind of statement is in the newspaper, the police will do something active about protecting him. I will certainly check up on that."

"He probably loves the attention," Anna said.

"That's a stupid thing to say," Tina said. "Considering that as his replacement, you don't even know him."

"I know the type," Anna said dismissively. "Their greedy little egos love anything that makes people look at them and think about them and worry about them."

"Shut up, Anna!" Adele said.

"Since I took his place here, a lot of you people have talked about this guy. I don't see why now we have to suddenly pretend everybody loves him."

Tina stood up. "I'm just not going to listen to any more of this stuck-up bitch's pontifications. The less she knows, the more she says." Tina walked out.

Adele felt tired of it all. She said, "What say we put a lid on uninformed speculation about Brian altogether." It was more than a suggestion.

Frances Tounley called back at eleven. "I think I've got the woman you want," she told Adele. "Donna Marie East. Aged twenty-two now. She's the only Donna East on record."

"That sounds about right."

"She's listed as having been born in De Gonia Springs."

"Wherever is that?"

"I don't have the faintest idea."

"But it's in Indiana?"

"Sorry. Yes, De Gonia Springs, Indiana."

"Go on."

"She first came to our attention when she was seventeen and had just had a baby. She said she was new to

Indianapolis, that her parents were dead and there was no one who could help her. She and the child were given public assistance after that. Then our records show the birth of twins about fifteen months after the first, the fourth ten months later and the fifth eleven months ago. All girls."

"Hang on, hang on!" Adele said. "I only know of two children."

"We show five: Billie, the oldest; Cindy and Sally, the twins; Mary Louise and Jeanette. All born on the public ward at Marion County Hospital. Mind you, our departmental financial support ceased before Jeanette's birth."

"Why was that?"

"There's a note that she was getting married and moving to St. Louis."

"And when was this?"

"She stopped claiming . . . more than a year ago. The last claim was for the week of January twenty-first, last year."

"What address do you have for her?"

Tounley read an address on Clayton Avenue, on the southeast side of town. "We visited in February last year, but Donna had moved. No forwarding address."

"Was there information on the father of the children?"

"None. The birth certificates list the fathers as unknown. That'll be nice for the kids when they grow up."

"I don't know about you," Adele said, "but I usually tell clients of mine to make up a name. But I'm sure you didn't hear me say that."

"Say what?"

Adele said, "I've been told that there is a man in Donna's life who supports her in anticipation of her receipt of an inheritance. You don't show anything about that, do you?"

"Nothing. Of course, not everything gets put into the

computer file. I can give you the name of her original worker, if you want to talk to him."

"All right."

"His name is Samuel Williams. Do you know him?"

"No."

"He doesn't work for us anymore, but I've got his home number, unless he's moved. I don't see any reason why he shouldn't be happy to talk to you." She read Adele the number.

"Many thanks," Adele said. Then, "I find it confusing about the other children, Frances. You don't have anything that might suggest why they aren't living with their mother, do you?"

"Nothing at all," Frances Tounley said.

From the telephone, Adele turned to the photocopy of King Smith's version of his conversation with Donna East. Immediately the children's names, Cindy and Sally, confirmed that Donna was the De Gonia Springs Donna East.

The document was the pouring forth of a woman whose feelings and life had been locked up by forces outside of her control, whose existence was confined and constrained by walls and by children, a woman who was desperate and passionate but who found the words to express her feelings hard to sort. But Adele also felt that she was reading about a woman who genuinely believed that her life would lead her to nothing good or kind or gentle.

There was little sign of any probing from Smith. He had acted solely as an aural receptacle for the flow of words, many of them about her childhood in a small town, of her departure with a floor-covering salesman who had set her up in a little apartment in Terre Haute—until his wife found out and she had to leave town.

She'd come to Indianapolis. Then she'd been "found"

by the man who had put her in the apartment she was in now, and who told her of this inheritance on which she had been pinning all her hopes, and even such dreams as she allowed herself.

Sally and Cindy were the only children mentioned, but there was one curious halting sentence: "Anymore, [stopped to cry] I can't even get myself [stopped to cry] no more babies."

Adele read the document slowly. She could not help but see the back porch of Donna East's apartment. She could not help but visualize the luxurious flowers and trailing growth of leaves that the porch must be in the summer and fall.

She could not but feel a dread for the fate of Donna East, wherever she was now.

18

ADELE called Proffitt to confirm the visit with Nora Harrington. Proffitt answered his phone, but his tone was surprisingly cool and formal.

They arranged to meet outside Harrington's just before one. "I'm afraid I can't stop now," Proffitt said. "I'll see you there."

They hung up, and Adele felt annoyed with the man. She had given him no sign that she wanted him to "stop." Had she? She'd called him Homer, but . . .

The irritation refused to dissipate and made it hard for her to settle to her paperwork. After all, Proffitt had been the one who asked her out. Now he talked as if she were chasing him.

Stupid man.

Stupid men.

What should have been the making of a simple arrangement had become an issue.

Or had it? Am I reading too much into "can't stop"? Perhaps it had been more to say something to someone at his desk than to her.

But Adele still felt restless.

126

So she went out. She had intended to visit Donna East's previous address anyway, the one given to her by Frances Tounley. It was part of Adele's own need to know about this missing woman.

Missing mother.

The Clayton Avenue address was a four-floor cement-block apartment building that looked solid but little cared for. The outside surface was stained with lichenous stripes following drip lines from the aging guttering; the mustache yard along the building front was bristly with dead brown weeds from last year's growth. Did Donna East never live anywhere nice?

The apartment buzzers, however, were all carefully labeled and the lock on the outer door was secure. Adele pushed the button marked "Superintendent." Within a minute a portly woman in grease-gray overalls opened the door.

"What you want, honey?" she asked.

"I'm trying to trace a woman and her children who used to live here. I'm hoping that you can help me, or that you will know someone else who can."

The woman's eyes narrowed.

"I'm a social worker," Adele said.

The woman eased the door farther open in order to examine Adele better. "Welfare?"

"No. I work for a private agency."

"ID?"

Adele showed the woman her agency identification and her union card.

The woman studied both carefully, then handed them back. "OK," she said. "Come on in. Let's do coffee."

The woman's apartment was at the back of the building on the first floor. She hesitated outside the door, and turned to Adele. She said, "My name's Karen. Do you like cats?"

Before Adele answered, Karen opened the door and went in.

The image of a gray kitten she'd had as a child came to Adele's mind. The kitten had been fearless and had died because it had strolled up to an irritable dog's food bowl. Irritation reminded Adele of Homer Proffitt. The dog had been a neighbor's. Called Rover. Homer. Rover. Homer. Rover.

Adele entered Karen's apartment. The presence of cat was overwhelming. It bombarded Adele's eyes, ears, and nose. Cat wallpaper, cat photographs, cat smell. And a seething mewl of the real things.

"Cats," Karen said expansively as she closed the door carefully behind Adele. "My weakness! Find yourself somewhere to sit."

Adele made friends while Karen made coffee. She made friends around her legs, and on her shoulders. She made friends in her lap. Some of the friends were large and languid. Three, beautifully mottled, were tiny, a few months bold. Another friend, a little older and pure black, jumped straight onto Adele's knees, ran up her chest and stuck its face up to Adele's, nose-to-nose.

"That's Sooty," Karen said, bringing the coffee. "She's a real character."

"How many do you have here?" Adele asked.

"Thirty-one."

Adele could not help showing her reaction.

Karen laughed easily. "I'm a real soft touch."

"Oh."

"No mice in my buildings!" It was an oft-repeated joke. Adele smiled.

"You don't like them, do you?"

"I'm . . . not used to quite . . ."

"I don't do things by halves," Karen said. "I get interested in plumbing, I become a janitor. I get fed up with my husband, I divorce all men. I take in a stray kitten . . ." She opened her arms, palms to the sky. "You can't fight your own nature, can you?"

"No," Adele said, "you can't."

Karen leaned toward her, examining her eyes closely for a moment. She said, "You've decided to like me, haven't you? I can see it."

"Yes, I like you."

"Good. Then I'll help you if I can."

She poured the coffee and handed Adele one of a pair of mugs with cats' faces fashioned into their sides. She took her own mug in one hand and found a kitten for the other. She sat on a floor cushion in front of Adele. She said, "What did you want to know?"

"About a woman named Donna East."

"A woman? A woman!" Karen laughed. "I'm a *woman*. Donna was a *child*. I don't just mean that she was young in years. She was a child. She always will be."

"You remember her, then."

Karen lifted an eyebrow and smiled and kissed the kitten. "I also like to know my tenants," she said, referring again to the excesses of her enthusiasms.

"How long was Donna East here?"

"Year and a half, or so. She left last January. I don't mean last month. A year ago."

"Do you know why she left?"

"She got mixed up with a highly suspicious man."

"Mixed up how?"

"How do they ever get mixed up with men?" Karen asked.

"She moved . . . to live with him?"

"I don't know. I don't know where she moved to." A sigh. An old affront. "This Clint didn't like me. He didn't know me hardly, but he made sure that Donna stopped talking to me."

"You met him then?"

"Oh yes. He came around doing polls, opinion polls."

"What kind?"

"Some bullshit about politics. I never believed him for a minute."

"What do you mean?"

"I mean I didn't believe he was really doing polls," Karen said. "He went round door-to-door all right, asking a few questions and writing the answers down. But I didn't believe it was the answers he was interested in then and I don't believe it now." She sniffed. "I mean, look: He came in here, asked me two things, did I like the mayor and what party did I vote for, and then he took off."

"If you didn't think he was a real opinion poll taker, what did you think he was?"

Karen put the kitten to her lips and *rrrrrr*ed her tongue to imitate a purr. "*I* think the poll thing was just a crack so he could look around."

"With a view to . . . ?"

"I don't know. Burglary? Most of us are poor around here, but that doesn't seem to stop them stealing from us."

"Have there been thefts, then?"

Karen shrugged. "Some," she said, but in a way that implied there had been no more than before. "I don't know. I don't *really* know what he was after, but it sure as hell wasn't opinions."

Karen paused.

Adele considered what had been said.

Karen said, "I'm pretty good at people." Smile. "I got you right, didn't I?"

"Yes."

"Well, this Clint spent an hour with Donna the first day. An hour! Do you know how long it would take to poll Donna East's political opinions? Two seconds."

Sniffed again.

"And two seconds was exactly how long this guy was here with me and with the others in the building. *Except* Donna."

Karen wagged her head, as if responding to a discomfort in her neck. She sipped from her coffee cat. She said, "Donna he talked to and he listened to and he flattered. And he *didn't* make a pass at, which is the first thing you might think he was doing up there. He didn't touch her. He didn't even try. And I know, because in those days Donna used to talk to me, and after he left her she came down and she was full of him."

"I see."

"She was also full of a child at the time. Might have had something to do with it." Karen paused, then looked up at Adele. "Do you know about the children?"

"I understand she had five."

"Well, this was the fifth, and the father was a goddamn sixteen-year-old who ran like a superstar when he found out what he had done. Mind you, at times a sixteen-year-old was a little on the mature side, conversationally, for Donna. She kind of looked up to him, if you know what I mean."

"I'm getting the picture."

"A sweet, sweet child, though," Karen said. "Don't get me wrong. She was a good 'un. She really was."

"Karen," Adele asked, "did Donna cope with the children?"

"Pretty good. She spent all her time at it and didn't do badly."

"I am here," Adele said, "because Donna is missing from where she's been living since she left you."

Karen studied Adele's face to assess the seriousness of the word *missing*.

"We have no concrete reason to think she's come to harm, but there are a number of strange circumstances."

"Such as?"

"For one thing, her neighbor says that since he moved into the room across the landing seven months ago, Donna's only had two children living with her, the twins."

"The poor lovely little mites."

"Then, sometime night before last, Donna and the two children suddenly left. I'm trying to get it sorted out. Do you know where she might have gone? Or what might have happened to the other three children?"

Karen shook her head solemnly. "I don't know about where she is, but to be without Billie and little Mary Lou, that strikes me as very funny."

"You don't know of anyone, a relative or something, they might be staying with?"

"No."

"And you don't know of anybody she might have gone to?"

"No." She added sadly, "If she'd wanted somewhere, she could have come here, of course. I'm sure she knows that I'd always be a friend."

Adele leaned back, carefully, and sipped from her coffee. She asked, "And this Clint? He came back?"

"The next day. And then every day till she moved out."

"Why?"

"I don't know. Though I can tell you, she'd have given him anything. Anything. Dressed up in plastic bags and acted like a week's shopping, whatever he might have wanted." Karen was struck by a memory. She said, "You know, my old man wanted it in a wheelbarrow once. Can you imagine me in a wheelbarrow?" She snorted.

Adele smiled with genuine sympathy.

"Almost right away this guy told Donna to stop talking to me," Karen said. She rubbed a finger back and forth across her tight lips. "So she did. I'd go up there, and she wouldn't even let me in. As far as I know, he stopped her talking to anybody. And two weeks later, she left."

"Did she give a reason?"

"She *said* that Clint was getting her a better place, and she said something about money that he'd found out that was supposed to be hers that she hadn't been getting. But I didn't believe any of that either."

"I see."

"On the day of the move, she didn't even say good-bye."

"Karen, can you tell me anything more about this Clint?"

"Like what?"

"Well, what he looks like, for one thing."

"Five eight. Skinny. Sandy hair. Kind of surprisingly baby-faced for a thin guy. Maybe thirty, thirty-five. Very . . . What can I say? Very *plausible* at first meeting. I mean *I* think he was a con man of some kind. But then I'm not a man fan these days." She turned to her kitten. "Am I, sugar? Baby. We haven't had a man in here for more than a year, have we? *Rrrrrr.*"

"You'd be able to recognize Clint if you saw him again?"

"Oh yes."

"Or saw a picture of him?"

"If it was a reasonable picture, I would think I could."

"This may be a police matter, Karen."

"Good," she said. "Anything I can do to put the bastard away, I'll do with a smile. Or how about having him *done*, eh, kitty? Shall we have the nasty man done?"

"Do you know anything else about him? Where he lived?"

"No."

"A phone number?"

"No."

"Any idea about how to trace him or contact him?"

"I did write down the license number of his car once. Now, where did I put that kitty? Where is the nasty man's car number? Oh yes. *Rrrrrr.*"

19

PROFFITT was waiting in his car outside Nora Harrington's house when Adele arrived at one-ten. He looked at his watch as he reached across the front seat to open the door for her.

Seeing him check the time reminded her that he had annoyed her earlier. "I operate punctually, Proffitt," she said crisply. "If I'm late there's always a good reason for it."

"I was late myself, ma'am," he said. "So what's been happening to you?" His friendly smile suddenly made it easy for her again.

So she told him about her visit with Karen the cat lady.

He listened attentively and nodded. Then told her the result of his telephone call to a prominent opinion research company.

"You're satisfied in your own mind that the polling company is bogus, then?" Adele said.

"Yes," Proffitt said.

They looked at each other. The shared question: Why make up a polling company?

"My first thought," Proffitt said, "was that taking polls

134

was a device to get into premises with a view to burglary. But I checked the scatter charts and talked to the burglary people in this Quadrant, and there's just no supporting evidence."

"I don't think it has to do with burglaries, either," Adele said.

"Do you have an idea, ma'am?"

"The guy ended up with Donna. So *I* would assume that he got what he went for."

"He went there to 'get' Donna East?"

"Maybe not Donna specifically. Maybe he was looking for someone like her."

"In what sense?"

"A woman alone. A woman without much going for her. No connections. Not much savvy. I don't know. You're a man. What would you want with Donna? That you couldn't get by leaving her where she was."

Proffitt considered.

Adele said, " 'Clint'—Jesus, picking a fake name like that tells you something about him, doesn't it?"

Proffitt said, "This Karen said Donna told her explicitly that the guy didn't come on to her?"

"Yes. But Donna stopped talking to Karen after a few days."

Proffitt shrugged. "And Donna wouldn't have minded anyway."

"That's what Karen says," Adele said. "Maybe it *was* sex. Think of that closet with the kids' beds in it," Adele said. "And the bolt on the outside. No need for a bolt unless things were going on that shouldn't be interrupted."

Proffitt nodded slowly. Then he said, "I had an idea about the other kids."

"What's that?"

"I wondered if maybe they died."

The looked at each other, sharing a moment thinking

about the poverty, the dependence, the confined nature of Donna East's life. Had there been more?

"I'll check when I get back to the office," he said. He gave his head a shake. "Maybe we got something on our hands here, ma'am."

Adele looked at his hands.

"Meanwhile, before we go talk to this Nora Harrington, let me call in that license plate number your cat lady wrote down." He looked at it. "Not from Indianapolis," he said.

"How do you know that?"

"It begins 'eighteen.' The first numbers code locations. I *think* that's Muncie. But we'll see what they can get for us by the time we get out of here."

Nora Harrington was an organized, capable young woman who tried to insist that having a physical disability was only incidental to her life. "I got things sorted out pretty good," she said as soon as her visitors were seated. "I got quite a good setup really. You'll see."

"We're not here to check on how you're coping or anything like that," Adele said. "This is Detective Proffitt from the police, and he wants to ask you some questions."

"Oh, I know what Mrs. McLarnon said when she called," Nora Harrington said. "But you people are *always* poking around. 'Are those dishes left from last night?' 'Is that a spider web on the ceiling?' "

"Not this time," Adele said.

Proffitt explained how the murdered man had been found, about the note on his body, and about the break-in at the agency. Then Adele described the man who had broken in.

"Doesn't sound like anyone I know," Nora said.

"Are you sure?" Proffitt asked.

"Someone luscious and big like that? I like 'em big. Yes, I'm sure." Then she asked, "Is there some reason that you thought I knew him?"

"Yours was one of the three files that we thought might possibly have been the one he was interested in," Proffitt said.

"Mine?" Nora smiled, surprised.

"It looked as if it might have been disturbed. So we wanted to check it out," Adele said.

"And another reason we've come to you," Proffitt said, "is because you used to have a social worker with the same name as the man who was murdered."

"I did?"

"Brian Wampler."

"Oh, Brian."

"That's right," Proffitt said.

"God, nothing's happened to Brian, has it?"

"He was perfectly healthy when I talked to him yesterday afternoon," Proffitt said.

"I saw him last week and he was in good form," Nora said easily. To Adele, "Well, you know Brian. Always joking and flirting and that."

Adele blinked. "You saw him last week?"

"Yeah."

"Where?"

"Here. Where do you think?"

"He came here?"

"Sure. He comes here. Well, not often, but sometimes."

"Since he stopped being your social worker?"

'Sure." Puzzled now. "I said that. He was here last week."

"Why did he come?"

Nora shrugged. "He is interested in how I'm getting on. He helped me set it all up, you know. He was just about the only social worker I ever met that made you feel he was really interested in *you*, you know what I mean?"

"Yes," Adele said. She spoke quietly.

"This new one, Miss McLarnon, she's all right, I guess.

But that's just it. It's 'Miss McLarnon' with her while with Brian it was always 'Brian.' I guess he did all the poking round that he had to do, but he didn't make you feel that was all he was here for. He was really interested, and he didn't stop being interested just because he works someplace else. That's what he says, you know?"

"So, his visits are social calls?"

"That's right."

"How many times has he visited since he changed jobs?"

"I don't know. Five. Six. He comes in the evening, on his way someplace else, that kind of thing. Look, is there something wrong, Mrs. Buffington?"

"I'm just surprised," Adele said. "I didn't know about it and I'm surprised."

"Nothing *happens*, if that's what you think. I won't say I wouldn't consider it, big handsome fella like that. But he hasn't offered and I'm not the kind of girl who chases a man." She laughed. "I don't have the equipment. Oh, Brian's all flirty and that, but it's just his way."

"I know." Adele said. "I know."

"There's nothing to worry about."

"I'm not. Please, be assured that I'm not."

"Well, what's the big deal then?"

20

"WHAT was the big deal about Wampler visiting her?" Proffitt asked as they sat in his car after leaving Nora Harrington.

"The big deal is that it is not done," Adele said forcefully.

Proffitt looked at her.

"It simply isn't done. A social worker who turns a case over to another social worker just doesn't continue to visit a client, and *certainly* not without clearing it with the client's new social worker."

"Who is the new social worker?"

"Tina McLarnon."

"And did she know about it?"

"I'm sure she would have mentioned it, but I'll check with her when I get back, of course." She wrinkled her face as she thought.

"It's more than that, isn't it?" Proffitt said.

She nodded. "It's puzzling."

"How?"

"Brian leaving the job with us was complicated. There was a case that I told you a little about, Sabrina Caldenwell, that he screwed up. He might well have been disciplined, but he quit instead. Only being Brian he wouldn't ever admit that he quit because of the case. He quit because he had a 'better offer.' "

"I see."

"And he *specifically* made a big deal about how he wasn't going to have to do any work at night in his new job."

"Ah. And now he makes unneeded visits at night voluntarily."

"Not just unneeded. Unprofessional. It really could do him harm if it were known. If he ever wanted to work with another agency, for instance."

"So why would he do it?"

"That's what I don't know," Adele said.

"Are we talking sex again?"

"It happens, I suppose."

"You mean between social workers and their clients?"

"There was a study in Minnesota that showed about a sixth of social workers, counselors and nurses admitted having had at least one sexual contact with a client either during or within three months of their professional contact."

"A sixth, huh?"

"Seventeen percent, if you're being fussy. Seventeen percent admitted it."

"And is that what you think is happening here?"

"Brian Wampler would plug a keyhole if he could do it without hurting himself and if he could tell somebody about it."

Proffitt smiled. "You really like this guy, don't you?"

Adele conceded the point. "Yeah," she said. "But honestly, I wouldn't have thought Nora would be the type he would have gone for. He'd know he had to keep it quiet, for one thing."

"The girl says nothing like that is happening," Proffitt said.

"And I believe her, so it must be something else," Adele said. "But I'll tell you this. Even without the rest of it, there is no way Brian Wampler would just visit Nora Harrington out of sheer sweetness, 'interested in how she's getting on.' That is not the Brian Wampler I know."

Proffitt lifted his eyes in thought.

"I thought that when he left I was finally finished with having to sort out his messes."

Proffitt let her fume. He turned to his police radio and asked about the result of his license plate check request.

The car for which Karen had written down the number was for a green and gold five-year-old Jaguar. The registered owner was an Elvis Mounty. The address was in Lynhurst, just south of Speedway.

Adele listened to the details with clear interest.

"You want to come?" Proffitt asked.

She looked at her watch. "Yes," she said, "but what I really have to do is sort out this business about Brian and his visitings."

"Looks like it's going to have to be dinner again, ma'am."

Adele breathed out heavily, paused, then smiled and said, "Yes. All right."

No sooner had Proffitt driven off than Adele remembered she hadn't asked him about De Gonia Springs. She pounded a fist on the passenger seat of her car. But it was anger with Brian Wampler rather than herself.

Patrick rose as Adele entered the office. His eyes were puffy. He looked . . . what? Unsteady?

Patrick said, "There was a call from a Sergeant Fleetwood, Adele."

"Thank you." Then, "Are you all right, Pat?"

"No," he said. "I'm being torn apart by love and I don't know what to do about it."

Tina was in the room, listening. Patrick obviously didn't care.

Adele looked at the pitiful young man. Twenty-two, not bad-looking. A nice boy, though somehow not knitted together.

Patrick said, "If she hates me so much, why did she encourage me in the first place?"

"Did she?"

He lowered his eyes. "Oh yes," he said. Passion dripped from the memory. "We went out, and, first time, we . . ."

"Oh." Adele touched him on his shoulder. "Suffering about love is not something that everyone is *able* to feel, Patrick."

"Why is she so awful to me?"

"As a person Anna is an awful girl."

"Sometimes I can't bear it. I keep thinking about her. I can't get her out of my mind. She obsesses me."

"Come into the office with me, will you?"

"OK."

A harmless, willing puppy of a man.

Would he like Lucy? Would Lucy like him?

"Tina," Adele said.

"Yeah?"

"Could you cover the switchboard? And then after Patrick takes it back, could you come in to see me?"

In the office Adele said, "What we call love is not always what it seems, you know."

"What do you mean?" Innocent. Open. Desperate.

"It doesn't always involve just your feelings for the person you think of as its object. There are all sorts of things going on. From your childhood and your relationship with your parents and how you feel about yourself in other ways . . ."

Patrick sat unresponsively. "I know what I feel," he said.

"I have a friend, a professional friend, I would like you to talk to," Adele said. "Will you do that?"

Patrick began to cry. "I've got to do something," he said.

Adele reached for the telephone.

Tina entered the office with some uncertainty. "What's it about?" she asked. "Is there some problem?"

"Tina, did you know that Brian Wampler has been visiting Nora Harrington?"

"Brian? Visiting Nora?"

"Five or six times over the last four months. He didn't clear it with you?"

"No." Then, "What's he want to visit Nora for?"

"She says it's just to see how she's getting on."

"Oh," Tina said. She shrugged. "Is that it?"

"I had a message you called," Adele said.

"That's right. Oh, hey, can you hang on a moment?" Carollee Fleetwood sounded hassled.

When she returned to the telephone she said, "You wouldn't believe what a madhouse it is here."

"Is that because Roy is away?"

"No, no. Him being here, shouting and pouting—that's all we need. No, it's just incredibly busy. At the moment it's kids who've run away. We've got four fourteen- and fifteen-year-olds, just in the last two days. If you see a kid walking alone on the street, grab it, will you? Chances are it's one of ours."

"Sure."

Fleetwood said, "I called because I wanted to let you know that I ran those names through our computer."

"Good."

"But I've come up with a blank. Nothing on a Donna

East. Nothing on a Clint Honneker, or a Hoosier Opinion Research Systems."

"I'm grateful that you took the time to try."

"How are you getting on?"

"The good news is that Homer Proffitt is working on it."

"Mmmm, tasty," Fleetwood said.

"But at the moment everything is getting very murky. For one thing, he's sure that there never was a polling company called Hoosier Opinion Research Systems."

"I see." Thoughtfully.

"For another it turns out that Donna East had five children in all."

"I thought you said there were two."

"Somehow, in the last year or so, three of them stopped living with her. At the moment we don't know where they went."

"Please don't tell me they're out walking the streets. We've got all we can handle here already, we really have," Fleetwood said.

"We think it's possible that they might have died."

"Oh."

"Homer is checking."

"Homer?" Fleetwood asked.

21

ADELE dialed the Hoosier Placement Center and asked the woman who answered if she could speak to Brian Wampler.

The woman said, "I'm sorry. Mr. Wampler is out of the office right now. But Mr. Williams is here, if you would like to speak to him instead."

Williams? The name rang a bell. "Who is Mr. Williams, please?"

"He founded the center. I'm sure he could help you."

"What's his first name, please?"

The woman was surprised by the question, but she said, "Mr. *Samuel* Williams."

"Did he used to be a social worker for the welfare department?"

"Why, I believe he did. Uh, who shall I tell him is calling?"

Samuel Williams, Donna East's former welfare worker. He ought to be talked to, seen. But first things first.

"Uh, no," Adele said. "I'm afraid it's Mr. Wampler that I need to speak to. I'll try his home. I have the number."

"Oh," the woman said, puzzled. "All right." Then she recovered: "Have a good one."

Adele fiddled on a notepad. She drew ivy leaves. She wrote Samuel Williams's name half a dozen times. Then she looked up Brian Wampler's home number and tried it.

Denise Wampler answered. Adele asked for Brian.

Speaking loudly, half laughing, Denise said, "No, no, no. Not here. But I expect him any minute, I really do."

Adele considered, and then decided to risk the trip. "I need to talk to him," she told Denise. "It's pretty important, so could you ask him to wait for me until I get there?"

"Sure, sure," Denise said. " 'Course. Anything I can do, anything." She made a funny sound that was a bit like another laugh.

The Wamplers lived in a former fire station just north of 16th Street. The conversion had made three small apartments out of the building and the brass fire pole had been retained, although moved to the front hall and stairwell. The building was called Firepole House.

When Denise Wampler opened the door, it was clear that she was verging on hysteria. Her expression was distracted. She spoke in a staccato shout. She gestured grandly. "Haha. Adele! Come in, come in!" Denise stepped back, seemed to lose balance with the sweep of her hand inviting Adele in, and she collapsed on the floor.

Adele stood over her for a moment. Denise was conscious and looking up. Adele offered her hands. Denise accepted. She allowed herself to be moved to a couch. She giggled quietly.

In the kitchen Adele took a few paper towels. She made a pad of them and moistened it with cold water. She brought it back to wipe Denise's face.

Denise was smiling broadly. "I fell down," she said. She giggled like a little child.

But the giggles turned to tears. "Brian was supposed to come home for lunch. But he didn't come. I made some sandwiches." Crying became shouting. "But the bastard didn't come home, and he didn't call, and he still hasn't come home and he still hasn't called."

She cried again.

Adele sat beside her and put an arm around her shoulder.

"Do you know there is some madman out there who wants to kill Brian?"

The image of the huge intruder standing in front of her, pointing and pushing with his thick finger, sent a tingling shiver through Adele's body. She said, "I've heard something about it."

"A policeman told Brian to be careful, but they couldn't protect him. How do you like that?"

Adele said nothing.

"Brian made a joke about it."

"It doesn't sound that funny to me," Adele said.

"I know Brian took it seriously, though. He took his gun," Denise said.

"What gun?"

"Brian has this twenty-two pistol with a long barrel. It's a target pistol really." She stopped in sudden thought. "Though he's never done any target shooting that I know of. Did he ever mention target shooting when he worked for you?"

"No."

" 'It's only little but it will do the job,' " Denise mimicked Brian's voice. "Shit!" she said. She cried again. The tears came in two big surges.

Adele mopped the woman's face.

"He doesn't come home much, Brian," Denise said. "Did you know that?"

How would I know something like that? "No," Adele said.

"He says that business is terrifically good."

"Business?" Adele asked involuntarily. "I . . ." She stopped.

"It is kind of a business, adoption. A private agency like that. They have to charge fees to pay the people that work for them."

Adele nodded, knowing that most "private" adoption agencies were charity-based and therefore financially subsidized. But yes, there were fees.

Suddenly Denise said, "I don't know why the fuck he married me. I really don't. He banged away day and night for the first few weeks, but now I hardly ever see him."

There was not a lot to say to that either.

"Probably just because he was afraid of AIDS, the bastard." She snapped her head back and forth. "Only he couldn't cut it. Couldn't survive with just the one woman."

Adele waited her out.

"I love him though," Denise continued. "For what it's worth." Abruptly she turned her face to Adele's. She said, "Did you know that my father is dying?"

"No," she said.

"Cancer." She nodded slowly. "Brian doesn't like to hear about it. I don't talk about it much." There was a pause. "It won't be long now."

"I'm sorry," Adele said as Denise began to cry again.

But she stopped crying abruptly to say, "I'll kill the bastard."

Adele was startled by the venomous force of the statement.

"Fucks around with my affections, and God only knows what else. Then drags it back in here. 'I'm so tired. I've been working so hard.' " A brief giggle. "I'll kill the swine and hang him up and cut off his quarters and make bacon out of him, I really will."

Adele wiped Denise's forehead.

"That feels good," Denise said in the calmest voice she had used. "Real good."

"Just lie back."

Denise lay back on the couch.

"Would you like a drink or something?"

"No. No. I'm all right."

"Good."

Adele sat by her as Denise closed her eyes. "You know . . . ?" Denise said.

"What?" Adele asked.

"I grew up on a farm."

"Did you?"

"My dad was a small farmer in Ladoga before he went bust."

"I didn't know," Adele said neutrally.

"We grew some corn and had some stock."

"Oh."

"So I *could* make the bastard into bacon. I know how."

22

ADELE stopped for a cup of coffee after she left Denise Wampler dozing on her couch.

Brian had not, of course, come home. Or called. Or sent a postcard. He *was* a bastard. Utterly thoughtless when it came to other people.

She shook her head.

Yet he was an adequate social worker, *except* for the reliance on "charm." He knew the law. He had a good grasp of how to analyze the structure of a situation and how to work out a plan to attack a set of problems.

Except sometimes.

Except, most notably, in the months before he left the Hendricks Agency. Except for Sabrina Caldenwell.

Adele sat up sharply at the table. She rocked her coffee cup.

"You like a refill?" the waitress asked.

"Jesus!" Adele said aloud.

"Pardon?" the waitress said.

Proffitt was at his desk the first time Adele called.

"What are you doing there?" she asked.

"Where else would you like me to be, ma'am?"

"I was sure you would be out."

"I've come back."

"So I gather."

"Did you want a rundown about this car?"

"That can wait for tonight," Adele said. "Can't it?"

"Yes," he said. "There's nothing dramatic."

"There's something I want to tell you."

"What's that, ma'am?"

"I've had an idea about why someone might have it in for Brian Wampler."

"OK," Proffitt said. "I'm primarily ears."

"Sabrina Caldenwell."

"Who would that be, ma'am?"

"A client. A case."

"That's not one of the three cases in the disturbed files, is it?" he said slowly.

"Forget the three disturbed files."

"OK, ma'am." He paused. "But you've mentioned the name before, haven't you?"

"Yes."

"It was the case Wampler quit over, wasn't it?"

"Sabrina Caldenwell was a young woman of twenty, an addict, who had a baby about ten months ago. She was single, without income. She was living near Dayton, Ohio, but came to Indianapolis to have the baby. The first anybody knew of her was when she turned up in labor at the Trauma Center at Methodist Hospital."

"Uh huh."

"Well, she had a baby boy and the doctor alerted Welfare because of the possibility the baby was addicted."

"As in heroin?"

"Yes."

"OK."

"Sabrina swore that she was off drugs, but the circumstances were vague enough, uncertain enough, that Wel-

fare carried the case the sixty days they're allowed to and
then they passed it over to us. It was allocated to Brian
Wampler."

"OK."

"For a while there didn't seem to be that much of a
problem. Welfare was almost sure Sabrina had broken the
habit and things were just about within what we would
call normal."

"Right. OK."

"Well, I gather that Brian spent a fair amount of time
with Sabrina, and it is certain that he did his charm number on her. And he got her to trust him, and he found
out various things like that Sabrina had come to Indianapolis to have the baby because she thought her mother
was here. Only when Sabrina got to the house she thought
her mother was living in, no mother."

"She moved or something?"

"It turns out that her mother had died eighteen months
before and Sabrina didn't know. Which, of course, had
done her mental state no good at all."

"Uh huh."

"Anyway, the key issue, as far as Sabrina was concerned, was that she wanted to keep the baby. It was a
repeated theme, virtually a preoccupation."

"OK."

"And, in fact, there is not a lot we can do in Indiana
to protect a baby who *might* be at risk. A baby can come
into a house where someone has killed five previous babies, but if that person is legally free, then we still can't
do anything preventive to protect the new baby. We've
got to wait until something happens to this one, too."

"What was the risk to the baby in this case?" Proffitt
asked.

"Basically the risk of neglect, if Sabrina went back on
heroin. We've seen a lot of that kind of thing, grievous
harm to infants where the mother is addicted. Enough

that these days we have a good chance of getting the child into some kind of care fairly early, *if* the mother is an addict."

"OK."

"So, the problem was the baby. Sabrina wanted to keep it, but also had no support of any kind. We can help, to a point, with money, but the real problem was the drugs. As an isolated woman, newly a mother, she was particularly vulnerable to feeling she needed them. And if she did, the baby would almost certainly be taken away at least for a while. She was desperate for that *not* to happen, since the baby was her only family."

"All right."

"But then, five months ago, she was busted with another junkie. Sabrina wasn't apparently high, but she had an ounce or so of street-grade heroin in her pocket."

"Where was the baby?"

"She had him with her. He was taken into a temporary care center while a conference was arranged to decide what to do."

"To what effect, ma'am?"

"The critical interview was before the conference. Brian went to talk to Sabrina, and in trying to maintain his 'good' relationship with her, she seems to have thought that he promised her that he could swing the conference to let her have the baby back under some kind of supervision."

"And it didn't happen?"

"The decision was that the child was to be kept in care while Sabrina's dependency was clarified. It wasn't a matter of her not having access to the child. It was just that the baby would live elsewhere, for the time being."

"OK."

"Sabrina was told. That night she overdosed."

"On heroin?"

"No. On a tranquilizer."

"And?"

"She was found, but quite a while afterward. She was just about alive. She still is alive. But the stuff affected her brain and her kidneys. She's pretty much a vegetable and she has no prospect of any quality of life at all."

"Oh."

"She left a note, Homer. It was barely literate and it was heartbreaking. The gist of it was that she said Brian had promised her that she'd be able to keep the baby, that he'd said he *loved* her and would take care of her and the baby. But that he had let her down."

"Loved her?"

"Brian vehemently denied any action or statement that could have suggested romantic attachment. Or promising her anything whatever about the baby. It might have been that she made it up, or that she heard what she wanted to hear, but it certainly is not something that can be settled easily or definitively."

"I see."

"One issue was why Brian didn't anticipate that she might harm herself, given how desperately she wanted the child. But as far as I am concerned it is a case of the Brian 'charm' being fatal, for all practical purposes. It was very, very ugly and awful, Homer. And it was clearly involved in Brian's decision to change his job. Although he always denied that, too. Et cetera, et cetera."

"Ma'am?"

"Yes?"

"What I'm wondering is the connection to the murder."

"I'm sorry. There is one. I got carried away."

"Tell me."

"We are working on the assumption that it was no accident that a man named Brian Wampler was killed. And that the break-in here was related to the murder. Well, I began to think about the cases Brian has been involved in that could have left someone with a sense of serious grievance. This case stands out from all his other cases here."

"And," Proffitt said, "Caldenwell is in A TO H."

"Right."

"What do you know about the father of the child?"

"I know that he was in a detox program they have in Ohio. It meant that while she was pregnant, he was away, out on a farm or something. Sabrina's file gives his name as George Nation."

"Well, well," Proffitt said.

"There's something else."

"What's that?"

"For an addict's baby, Sabrina's son was extremely large when he was born."

23

"Just who is this Homer Proffitt?" Lucy asked her question coyly. She stood in the doorway of the bathroom.

Adele lay in the steamy tub. Without opening her eyes she went to what she thought was the heart of the question: "If it puts too much pressure on you to iron the things you need for tonight and tomorrow *and* make yourself food, just tell me what you'd like and I'll make it for you in a few minutes."

"It's not that," Lucy said.

Adele opened her eyes.

"All of a sudden it's Homer this and Homer that. Dinner every night. I thought that you had a serious relationship with Albert. Or is that all over now?"

"Of course not." What a funny question, considering that Albert was here this morning. "Although I shouldn't have to remind you that Albert doesn't own me."

"I know." Lucy dropped her eyes.

Shyness now? Or is something going on?

Adele said, "Homer Proffitt is a policeman, and suddenly at the agency we have two cases that involve the police and he happens to be working on both of them."

"So you have to go out with him every night?"

"I'm eating dinner with him because it's a convenient time to talk."

Lucy shrugged.

"Most of our conversation is about business, and I pay for myself."

"You pay for yourself with Albert."

"That's different."

"But why do these so-called police cases need *you* to do so much?"

"They involve people who have worked for me. They involve agency clients. And although you may have forgotten, I was the victim of a crime night before last."

"But he didn't do anything to you, did he?"

"You don't have to be murdered to be a victim, love."

"No, I know." Eyes down again.

"Lucy, is there something you want to talk to me about?"

"Not especially. But . . ."

"But what?"

"Anymore you seem to be an absentee mother."

When she's tense she sounds more Hoosier. Something is going on.

"Absentee mother, for a twenty-one-year-old?" Adele asked it in as kindly a way as she could.

"A twenty-one-year-old raised without a father. A mother is bound to be more important to someone in my position than for most people."

Gently, "When it suits you."

"Thanks very much."

"That's not meant to be a criticism, love. But there's something on your mind. I do wish you'd say what you want to say to me."

Looking at the floor, Lucy said, "I'm thinking about moving into my own apartment."

"Oh."

"Is that all you have to say? 'Oh'?"

"Give me a chance."

"You're angry, aren't you?"

"No."

"Well, what then?"

"I don't know what I think. Is it . . . Is it that you want to move in with Fritz?"

"I don't think so. Well, maybe, but that's not it. I just don't feel so comfortable here now. I feel you're watching all the time."

Having been cross-examined about Homer Proffitt, Adele wondered who was watching whom, but she said, "You know the top floor is yours."

"Yes."

"And you can have whoever you want"—oooh, poor choice of words—"to visit."

"I know," Lucy said. "But that doesn't mean that I'm comfortable."

I can understand that, Adele thought. "I can understand that, love."

"Can you?"

"Sure." Then, "How far have you gotten in your plans?"

"Not very."

Adele thought about money, what she had in savings. "But you like the idea?"

With more animation Lucy said, "Sometimes when I think about it, it seems great. But then when I think about you going out with strange men, I worry about you living alone."

Adele laughed.

"Don't laugh at me."

"Come here, little daughter," Adele said. She sat up and extended a hand.

Lucy came to her and Adele pulled her down and kissed her on the forehead and got her wet. "You know how much I love you," she said.

"I guess."

"When you want to live somewhere else, I'll do everything I can to make it possible."

"Will you?"

Be careful. "Which is never to say that you won't be welcome here whenever and for however long you want."

Lucy dropped her eyes yet again.

Adele asked, "Is something wrong?"

"I didn't say that for sure I wanted to move. Just that I was thinking about it."

"And I didn't say that I wanted you to move, either. Just that if it's what you want, I'll help."

"Thanks," Lucy said. "I'm going to do my ironing now."

"OK."

But Lucy turned back in the doorway. "What the hell kind of name is *Homer*, for gosh sakes? Nobody is named Homer anymore."

"My daughter says that nobody is named Homer anymore," Adele said as they sipped Chinese tea.

"Perceptive girl," Proffitt said. He leaned to one side and rubbed the back of his head and neck. He looked tired. He said, "To tell the truth, my born name was Throckmorton."

"Sure."

"After that guy in the old radio program, *The Great Gildersleeve.* Do you remember it?"

"Too young," Adele said.

"Me too, but my pa loved him. This Throckmorton P. Gildersleeve guy owned a drugstore and had this nephew that got up his nose all the time, nephew called Leroy."

Adele smiled.

"So," Proffitt said, "when I came along my dad naturally called me Throckmorton."

"Naturally."

"But then, see, the kids in first grade got to teasing

me so bad that I started calling myself Homer."

"Mmmmm."

"Seemed a more normal, down-home name. Changed it legally when I was twenty-one."

"Am I supposed to believe all this?"

"Doubt is, of course, your prerogative, ma'am." Proffitt smiled and put both hands behind his head and leaned back and stretched and yawned. "Oooo-eee. You city gals."

"Homer, there's something I've been meaning to ask you," Adele said.

"I am not married, ma'am. Nor am I emotionally encumbered. Not anymore."

At this she laughed. "Not the question I had in mind."

"So sorry to hear that," he said, but his eyes twinkled, if anything.

"You're in a funny mood tonight."

"Could be, could be."

"Is there any special reason?"

"Just overcome by the sparking electric sizzle of your presence, ma'am. And maybe a little fed up with my life. All I ever seem to do is work."

"Sounds like the Friday frazzles to me."

"I would much prefer a more romantic diagnosis of what ails me. Despairing dynamic detective desires delectable . . ."

Dishy damsel? "Dinner?"

"If you say so."

Thinking of d's: "Homer, there was something I forgot to ask you this afternoon," Adele said.

"My knowledge is at your command."

"Do you know a place called De Gonia Springs?"

Proffitt's eyes narrowed. "The little town near Boonville?"

"You know it?"

"It's down near home."

"Well, well."

"May I ask the significance?"

"De Gonia Springs," Adele said, "is where Donna East told Welfare she was born."

"Is that so?" Proffitt said. His manner sharpened immediately.

"Is it near Evansville?"

" 'Bout twenty miles east," he said. "You know, I once met a farming family by the name of East out that way."

"The hell you did!"

"Yes, ma'am."

"Could that have been Donna's family?"

"If she came from De Gonia Springs, it could. Or relations."

"She might keep in touch."

"She might." Proffitt considered. "I think maybe I'll see if I can get a number and give them a call."

"Good."

"Yes," Proffitt said. He nodded. He stopped. He said, "Unless, ma'am, you might be partial to a little drive down that way yourself."

"A drive?"

"To De Gonia Springs. You could talk to the parents—if that's what they are—yourself. And then we could spend a few minutes looking round Evansville. Quite a place, my hometown. It's got some real nice done-up riverfront mansions on the Ohio. Mesker Park Zoo and Amusement Park. Wesselman Woods. Ma'am, I reckon Wesselman Woods, at two hundred and five acres, is just about the largest tract of virgin timber within the boundaries of a city anywhere in the United States."

"I'm sure it is, Homer."

"I thought maybe if we set off real early tomorrow morning, I could show you around and still not get back too late. Or, if you don't like to get up quite so early, well, we can always stay over."

"I'm not afraid of getting up early in the morning."

"Now there's a pity, ma'am."

Adele looked at him.

He looked at her.

"Is this a serious suggestion?" she asked.

"Sure is."

"Well, I don't know, Homer."

Proffitt nodded. "Sounds like you got real good judgment, being careful about driving off with a fella got the born name of Throckmorton."

Food came.

They ate in silence until Adele said, "Tell me about the Jaguar and Elvis Mounty."

"Nice little guy," Proffitt said. "He has a shoe store in Speedway. He's been saving to buy a Jag for thirty years and finally got it for Christmas."

"So he wasn't the owner last January."

"Nope. The owner last January was a Steven Julian Fawcett. I stopped round that address too, but I found out he's dead."

"Oh."

"Died three years ago, but *his* Jag was totaled by his son about six months before that. In fact what we turn out to be dealing with here is a stolen car with recycled documents."

"So where did Mr. Mounty buy it?"

"From an ad in the paper. There was a telephone number and the man brought the car over to show him. But that man was the second owner after the time we're interested in. I've got the department car people working on it all. But I'm not expecting a whole lot in the way of results."

"Oh."

"Not quick anyhow."

"And for sure we're not going to get a real name for Clint Honneker out of it."

"That's a shame."

"Yes, ma'am."

Proffitt looked at her. "I do have some other information for you."

"What do you mean?"

"I also talked to the head of our computer information system, a captain called Tidmarsh, and he seems to be quite a heady guy."

Adele waited.

"After I explained what we were working on, he agreed to look me out some information about George Nation."

Sabrina Caldenwell's boyfriend. "What did he find?" Adele asked.

"George Nation was released from his detox program two weeks ago last Monday."

"No kidding."

"It doesn't prove anything."

"But it certainly keeps him as a possible."

"I'm getting a copy of the full files on him from Ohio. It'll probably be ready for me when I get back to the department."

"You're going back tonight?"

"I expect so. It won't keep me from getting up early in the morning, if that's your worry."

"It wasn't my worry."

"A fella wants to make his mark, he's got to spend a lot of time drawing."

"I'm sure."

"I tried to find out what size of man this George Nation is, but I couldn't get anyone on the phone who'd worked with him. Still, that will come with the full records."

"Homer, have you told Detective Diehl about Nation?"

"I didn't see Diehl all day, ma'am."

Adele stared at Proffitt, trying to understand. Then, a missing link, she asked, "Did you read the newspapers?"

"The newspapers?"

"Today."

"No, ma'am. Why?"

"Because they say that police think the killer may have murdered the wrong man."

"Do they now?"

"You seem to be reacting rather calmly."

"How should I be reacting?"

"Doesn't publishing that as a speculation put Brian Wampler in more danger?"

"The killer still doesn't know where your Brian Wampler lives."

"He's had more time to find out."

"I am not unmindful of the danger, ma'am. What I have done is have a word with a few of the guys who are out on patrol tonight. So we've got special attention being given, first, round your office."

"My office?"

"If it's where he went for the address before . . ."

The idea of someone, *that* huge man, entering her agency branch, again! Adele's heart speeded up.

"Second, I've got some other guys giving extra attention to the area of Brian Wampler's house."

Adele considered. "Extra attention. Will that be enough?"

"I'm not the only man in the Indianapolis Police Department who has an ambition or two, ma'am. I tell a couple of patrolmen they've got the chance of something lively happening, they'll put some effort into it."

"You sound pretty sure."

"I used to be on patrol myself," Proffitt said.

"I see."

"I also tried to telephone Wampler before I came here, just to make sure he's taking it seriously."

"I know he's carrying a gun," Adele said. "His wife told me. A twenty-two target pistol."

"He could empty a twenty-two twice into a guy the size you said and still not stop him."

"What did Brian say to you?"

"Nothing. He wasn't home from work, and what must be the wife said she didn't know when he was due back."

"Still not home?"

"What do you mean, 'still,' ma'am?"

"He was expected for lunch and didn't show up. I was over there for a while this afternoon and his poor wife was a wreck."

"Now you mention it, she did sound a little funny."

"Oh, Homer!"

"I'm sure nothing has happened," Proffitt said. But he took the napkin off his lap and signaled to the waiter for his bill.

24

THEY drove in Proffitt's car, and although they didn't speak, the shared tension grew the closer they got to Wampler's address.

When Proffitt pulled up down the street from Firepole House a little after seven-thirty he asked Adele, "Which floor do they live on, ma'am?"

"Downstairs, on the left."

Lights were on.

"I think we best have a quick look around outside before we go to the door."

Adele nodded and said, "All right."

"Stay behind me, OK?"

"Yes."

They left the car and walked to the Wamplers' side of the building. They avoided the streetlight outside the house. Nothing inside the house was visible; curtains were drawn at all the windows.

"Do you know what kind of car or cars they might have, ma'am?"

"No," Adele said.

Proffitt looked toward the back of the building and at the surrounding land and shrubbery.

166

Suddenly they heard a woman shriek. The sound was from inside the Wamplers' and it was a sound of pain. The shriek was followed by crying.

"Come on, ma'am."

They ran to the front of the building. Proffitt drew his gun. "Get off to the side," he said. Adele stepped back to the corner they'd just come around. "If there's trouble," he said, "go to my car and get us some help. The radio is lying on the front seat. It's the red button on the side. Just push it and talk."

"All right."

Proffitt tried the outside door. It was locked. He considered ringing the bell, but as he did so there was another cry from inside. He stepped back to kick at the door.

As he lifted a foot, a man's voice said sharply, "Stop right there, bud!"

Proffitt froze, then lowered his foot.

"I've got a gun on your gut, and if you make one teeny weeny move with that thing in your hand, you're history."

The voice came from a shadow in a recess at the front of the building where the fire-truck doors used to be.

Proffitt held his position motionless.

"Nice and easy now, let's work our finger away from the trigger so you're holding the thing by the butt."

Proffitt hesitated.

"Do it!"

He did as he was told.

"Tell the woman to step out where I can see her."

Proffitt said nothing, but after a moment Adele stepped clear of the building.

"Now, bud, easy does it. Let's get the gun on the ground. Slowly. Gently. Don't drop it. We don't want any nasty accidents. Keep your arm stretched out straight where I can see it."

Proffitt held his gun at arm's length in front of him and lowered it a little. He said, "I am a police officer."

"And I'm Madonna. You get the piece on the ground, sunshine, or what you are is a piece of Swiss cheese."

"I am Detective Sergeant Homer Proffitt."

There was only silence from the shadows.

"Are you Gammage, or are you Martyniuk?"

More silence.

Another pause.

"I talked to you on the phone earlier this evening. I asked you to keep an eye on this house."

The silence continued. Then, abruptly, a uniformed patrolman stepped from the shadows holstering the gun. "Christ, Proffitt, we nearly had us an embarrassing little incident there."

"I heard screams from inside the house," Proffitt said. "I was going in."

"Hell, they been coming on like that for fifteen minutes, ever since some man went in," Martyniuk said. "I was driving by, saw him. Remembered what you said, so I been hanging around a little. He went in with a key, so I figured he wasn't an intruder. And if you listen up a little I reckon you can tell it's just domestic."

"All right," Proffitt said. "I'll ring the bell. You hang back."

"OK."

Proffitt rang the bell.

After several moments, Brian Wampler answered the door.

"The bastard, the bastard, the bastard!" Denise Wampler intoned.

"I've been out working!" Wampler insisted. "My job doesn't stop just because some guy with my name gets himself killed."

"I think the situation has become a little more than just that, Mr. Wampler," Proffitt said.

"Bastard! The lying bastard leaves me rotting here all

day while he's out fucking some woman! Not a phone call! Not a message! Nothing. Nothing!"

The doorbell rang.

The sound seemed a relief to Wampler, who went to answer it.

While he was out of the room, Denise Wampler said to Adele, "He *told* me he was done with the catting around. He *said* he wanted to settle down. Have kids. Be a *normal* person." A shower of tears became a cloudburst.

Wampler returned and said, "There's a policeman outside who wants to talk to you, Detective."

Proffitt left as Denise Wampler's wrath returned to its object. "Bastard! Bastard!"

"She loves an audience," Wampler said to Adele.

"Don't involve me in your private wars, Brian."

"You involved yourself," he said irritatedly. "You came here this afternoon, and you're here again now." He sniffed, not without fatigue. "Must be love," he said.

"I have business with you," Adele said.

"What's that?" he asked easily.

"Bastard! Bastard! I gave up a perfectly good man for you." Denise pulled at one of Adele's shoulders. "I had a fiancé. A lawyer. I would have been happy!"

"It's obviously going to have to wait till tomorrow," Adele said.

"But it's Saturday tomorrow," Wampler said.

"Lying, fucking, lying, play-around, juvenile, half-assed bastard! It doesn't matter what I do for you or how I do it, it's not enough!"

"Tomorrow," Adele said. Her tone allowed no contradiction. "In the morning. Ten o'clock, at the office."

"What the hell is this about?"

"It's about Nora Harrington."

"Who's that?" Denise asked, suddenly attentive.

"No one," Wampler said.

"One of your floozies? Some poor waitress or secretary or sales assistant or nurse or receptionist or social worker whose life you're ruining in double quick time?"

Wampler turned to face his wife and said, "Nora Harrington is a goddamn former client who's short one arm and both legs, but for all that she manages to get through life without being a goddamn bitter neurotic shrew!"

Turning to Adele, Denise said, "If you had to put up with what I have to put up with, you'd be a shrew, too!"

At that moment Proffitt returned to the room and everyone turned to him.

"Ms. Buffington, Patrolman Martyniuk just heard on the radio that a man's been arrested outside the Hendricks Agency office."

"Good heavens!"

"He's being taken in. I think we should go downtown."

As they drove Adele worked something out.

She said, slowly, "Homer, it was *you* who told the newspapers that the killer might have got the wrong man, wasn't it?"

Proffitt said nothing.

"It couldn't have been anybody else. Nobody on Diehl's team is following that line of thought. It had to be you."

Proffitt said nothing.

"My God!" Adele said.

"It seemed like it might be a way to wrap this up quickly."

"By putting Brian at greater risk."

"I don't think it did," he said. "Not a whole lot."

"Even going out to dinner with me was a way of making sure I stayed clear of the office, wasn't it?"

Proffitt paused. Then he said, "Things never don't have to have just the one reason for the doing of them, ma'am." But the affected folksiness came across as charmless and insensitive, and they sat in silence for the rest of the journey.

Proffitt parked in the police garage and they walked quickly up the corridor to the main hall in the basement. They took an elevator to the police interrogation rooms on the fourth floor.

Two young patrolmen rose from wooden chairs as Proffitt entered, and they greeted him with big grins. Proffitt shook hands with both of them and followed them into an office where, it was made clear, Adele was not to follow.

After a few moments Proffitt returned. He looked reflective rather than celebratory.

"They don't know the man's name," he said. "He's refused to say anything. All that happened was that he was behaving suspiciously outside the office, looking in the windows, trying the door. When they approached him he became abusive."

"Is he big? Do you want me to look at him?"

"He's not big."

"Oh." Adele blinked.

"He's a guy about fifty, wiry build, funny little beard, and he was carrying a cane with a head on top."

25

KING Smith was huddled in a corner of the interrogation room. He didn't look up as the door was opened.

"Mr. Smith?" Adele asked.

Smith's head jerked toward her. His eyes were bright and caught the light from the doorway. "You!" he said. He snorted. "So, they've got all the straightjacketing forces of social organization conspiring together to bear down for the kill," he said. He shook his head forcefully from side to side. "This is goddamn Kafkaesque!"

After a few minutes King Smith allowed Proffitt to lead him to the detective's squad room.

Proffitt took several minutes to explain how two police officers came to be watching the Hendricks Agency office and why they had taken him into custody so quickly.

Smith did not accept the explanation graciously. When he did speak he said, "All I was trying to do was find out if anybody was in there."

"I see," Proffitt said.

"Sometimes when I walk by at night there's a light, somebody working late. But I'd hardly been there for a minute when these two fucking great blue monsters jumped me. What are they? Colts rejects? I've never seen cops that big before."

Adele glanced at Proffitt, who clearly had so many "ambitious" patrolmen to select from that he could take the size of a possible arrestee into account. A vision of a city patrolled by hundreds and hundreds of policemen wanting nothing more than a big hit, a spectacular arrest.

"Why did you want to see someone?" Proffitt asked.

"I had something to say to someone," Smith said snottily.

"Was it a specific person you wanted to talk to, or would anyone have done?" Proffitt asked.

Smith looked at Adele, suddenly furious. "It wasn't your goddamn Anna bitch I was after," he said. "Told him all about that, have you? Well think what you fucking well want to, but I'm not a goddamn cunt hound. I have other things on *my* mind, even if *you* don't."

"Mr. Smith," Proffitt said, "I haven't been told any story about you or anyone named Anna."

"I bet! And the goddamn cops there didn't jump me either, huh?"

"I've explained the circumstances that led to Patrolman Harris being a little quicker to bring you in than in other circumstances he might have been."

"The fascist hit me. Did he tell you that?"

"And you were abusive and threatened him with your cane."

"I'll sue this city for every last domed stadium."

"Of course, that kind of decision will be one you can consider at your leisure."

"Damn right."

"But sir, if you have something you wanted to tell Ms. Buffington, then we'd be grateful if you would do that so we can see about expediting your release."

Smith paused and looked from one to the other, seeking maximum dramatic effect. He said, "I had a telephone call from Donna East a little while ago and I thought you ought to know about it."

He got his reaction.

Adele jerked forward with attention.

"But since I never got your name and therefore couldn't get a telephone number, I went down to your office to see if I could make contact through someone there."

"You've actually talked to Donna East?" Adele asked.

"That is what I said, wasn't it?"

"What did she say?" Adele asked.

Smith took a breath and settled to remember. "She didn't talk for very long."

"Oh," Adele said.

"But she sounded upset."

"What exactly *did* Donna East say, Mr. Smith?" Proffitt asked.

"She said that she got my number from Information and she had to talk quietly. But she was so nervous that she didn't really lower her voice much at all."

"Did she say where she is?" Adele asked.

"What exactly did she say?" Proffitt asked again, overriding Adele's question.

"She said that it wasn't like she was told it was going to be," Smith said. Then he leaned back. "Look, with a little concentration I can probably give it to you just about word for word."

"You can?" Proffitt asked.

"She knows," Smith said. "I have this thing."

Adele nodded. Proffitt didn't ask for further explanation.

Smith concentrated. He closed his eyes. His voice took on a higher pitch when he was repeating words for Donna East. " 'Mr. Smith, is that you?' I said it was. 'This is Donna, Mr. Smith, from across the door.' "

"Across the door?" Proffitt.

"That's what she said."

"Go on."

" 'Donna,' I said, 'I've been worried about you.' 'I'm getting worried about me too, Mr. Smith.' 'What's happened, hon?' 'I'm being kept in a big brick house, only in a lock room, and what's happening isn't what he said was supposed to.' 'What's that?' 'Wait a sec. I thought I heard a noise. Just a sec.' 'Donna, are you there?' "

Smith paused and breathed heavily. His eyes remained closed.

Neither Proffitt nor Adele spoke.

"Then, when she came back to the phone, she was even edgier," Smith said. "She said, 'I didn't know nobody to call but you, Mr. Smith. I got your number from the information. There's this phone in the room across the hall when they didn't lock the door this time. But I got to talk quiet. I don't know why they're doing it, or rightly what's happening, Mr. Smith. But they was god-awful angry when I said about me being sterilized now and they've gone and took Cindy and Sally away, and I'm purely petrified about they're all right. Mr. Smith, it's not like it's supposed to be. I'm supposed to have a job and get this heritance. That's what Clint said and that's why I come with him. But now I'm here when I ask about the job they just look sour shit at me all the time and say they don't know what they're going to do with me. I've come over all scared, Mr. Smith, cause I ain't never heard people talk about a person the way the one of these guys is talking and he is talking about me! And . . .' "

Smith stopped.

"And what?" Adele asked

"And nothing. She stopped there. We were cut off."

26

Proffitt said nothing and seemed to be deep in thought.

"I didn't know your name, see?" Smith said to Adele. "But I thought that someone ought to be told about it."

"Oh yes," Adele said.

"She sounded very frightened."

"I understand."

"I didn't *ask* the woman to call me," Smith said. "And God knows I don't have the time to take from my work to get involved, but I didn't want the responsibility of not telling anybody about it. So I went down to your office."

"You could have called the police," Adele said.

"Huh!" Smith said as dismissively as he could with a short sound. "I *might* have called the police, but I didn't know they knew anything about Donna, did I? You didn't tell me that you had involved the police, did you?"

"All kinds of thing are happening at a speed I just can't keep up with, Mr. Smith. This is only one of them. The last couple of days have been like nothing else in my life."

Smith shrugged. "I am not interested in *your* problems, Ms. Buffington."

Homer Proffitt ended his reflections and turned to face the two of them. "Mr. Smith," he said.

"Yeah?"

"Is what you've just told us the truth?"

"What the fuck kind of—"

Proffitt raised a finger. It seemed, somehow, menacing. "Is it the truth?"

"Yes."

"If so," Proffitt said, "I think that you are in a lot of danger."

"What? Me?"

"I'm going to ask you to wait here until I get one of our captains to come in. When he arrives I'll explain what I mean about your being in danger. Please be a bit patient. I'll get a captain here as fast as I can. What I would like you to do in the meantime is to dictate what you have just told us onto a tape. Do you think you could do that?"

"Are you serious?"

"I couldn't be more serious, Mr. Smith. Can you remember the conversation again and tape it?"

"Sure. I explained to the lady here that I've got a kind of brain that—"

"All right. I'll get someone to bring in a tape recorder. Just stay here."

Proffitt left.

"What's he mean, in danger?"

"I don't know," Adele said.

Adele found Proffitt in the squad room while the tape recorder was being set up for Smith in an office. "Homer," Adele said, "what do you mean he's in danger?"

"Can you hang on for that explanation until the captain gets here?"

"If I have to."

"What would help most is if you would go in there and tell me whether what Smith says is the same as he told us."

Captain Graniela was a stocky man, but he bragged that his bulk was all muscle. Certainly he worked hard on his personal fitness. He even kept weights and an exercise bike in his department office.

When he received the call from Proffitt he was about to sit down to dinner with business friends. He was not pleased to be interrupted, and he left the dinner table saying "It better be a mass murder."

What Graniela said when he met Proffitt at the elevator door was, "This better be some hot shit, Detective."

Proffitt led him to the interview room and introduced Adele and Smith. Ignoring them, Graniela said, "Get on with it."

Proffitt explained the history of Donna East, as they knew it.

Graniela grew impatient. "So, you got a missing woman and her kids is what you got, as far as I see."

"There is no official record of the three missing children, Billie, Mary Louise or Jeanette, having died in Indiana," Proffitt said. "And there's no record on any of them in the city education department's computers."

Adele was momentarily startled. Proffitt hadn't mentioned the result of his checks of death records or even that he had thought to look for evidence of schooling.

"And then," Proffitt said, "tonight Donna East called Mr. Smith."

"So she ain't even dead," Graniela said.

Proffitt turned to Smith. "Shall I play the tape or can you recall the conversation for Captain Graniela?"

"I can recall the conversation."

"OK. If you would."

Smith recited the conversation as he had twice before.

Graniela listened carefully. When Smith had finished, the captain turned to Proffitt again. His face showed displeasure. "What is this guy? A parrot?"

"He has a knack for remembering conversations," Proffitt said. "The aural equivalent of a photographic memory."

Graniela looked at Smith. "Aural, huh?" he said. "So, a missing person who calls in, or a kidnapping where the victim agreed to go with the people who took her wherever she is. What else you got for me, Proffitt?"

Proffitt said, "Sir, even apart from the three unaccounted-for children, my instinct tells me that this is a serious case. If that's right, let's think about what happened at the end of the telephone call that Mr. Smith received."

Graniela waited.

"Donna was interrupted, having already expressed fear about being overheard. So let's assume she was taken off the phone forcibly and that the people she is with are malevolent."

"Malevolent," Graniela mimicked.

"What will they be doing to her? I think they'll go at Donna hard to find out who she was calling and why. And I think Donna will tell them sooner or later, and probably sooner."

Graniela couldn't, offhand, think of anything sarcastic to say about this line of reasoning.

Everyone looked at Smith.

"If these people are malevolent," Proffitt repeated, turning back to Graniela, "they will then think about whether what Donna told Mr. Smith poses them any danger."

"Well?" Smith asked.

"They will also get from Donna the fact that this is not the first time she has contacted Mr. Smith. *I* say that the chances are good that they will want to have a look at

Mr. Smith themselves, that they will want to talk to him to evaluate what kind of risk he might be for them. I also say that they are going to want to do that immediately."

"You want a stakeout at his house, that it?" Graniela asked.

"A little more," Proffitt said. "I want to return to the building and go to his apartment as if I am him."

Graniela sighed.

"I'm about the same height, and with his outer clothing I ought to be able to pass on the street. I figure chances are good that they've already been in his apartment and found he isn't there. And I figure they're waiting there now."

"That's what you 'figure,' is it?" Graniela asked.

"That's it. It's not a certainty, by any means, but if there's a chance to get them, or some of them, we must act decisively. And that's why I asked you to come back to the office, sir."

Graniela worked his jaw, and sucked the inside of each cheek in turn. He said to Smith, "Please don't mind me saying so, but you look kind of ragtag, fella."

"I don't like suits and ties," King Smith said.

"What do you do for a living, Mr. Smith?"

"I am a playwright."

Graniela blinked. "A—"

"Playwright," Smith filled in for him. "I write plays."

"Jesus mother of God!" Graniela said.

There was silence until Graniela said, "So you could have made all this stuff up."

"I didn't."

"Do you know what happens to people who jerk us off?"

"I don't have to take this kind of abuse," Smith said. "I'm a perfectly respectable and responsible citizen. I pay my taxes." He stood up.

"Sit down!" Graniela shouted.

Smith sat down.

"People who jerk us off have their tiny testicles run over one by one by every police car in the city."

Smith said nothing.

"I don't like it," Graniela said. "I think it stinks." He paused. Nobody spoke. He turned to Proffitt. "But if you want some rope to hang yourself with, country boy, then you got it."

27

GRANIELA authorized the assignment of one late-shift Homicide detective and two patrolmen. The patrolmen were taken off George Sector, the closest to headquarters, and during the time it took for them to come in, Proffitt found a concealed microphone/transmitter that worked; the first two he tried did not. He met his team in the Homicide/Robbery office on the second floor. Adele and King Smith came with him.

Proffitt explained what he wanted as briefly as he could. He offered the minimum information about the case the suspects were involved in, "a possible kidnapping." No, he didn't know how many of them there would be. No, he didn't know what they looked like. No, he didn't know how dangerous they were, but they must be assumed to be bad: Donna East had never heard anyone talk about a person the way one of them had talked about her.

He did think that by now the suspects would already have arrived at Smith's apartment, that they would have entered it and found it empty, that they would be waiting.

Waiting where? "They don't know Mr. Smith, so my bet is that they'll be inside in the apartment. If not in the apartment itself, then in the apartment across the hall."

"So we all go gangbusters?" Patrolman Mazur asked.

"No," Proffitt said. "I go in alone, with you guys close. If they do take me for Mr. Smith, I want to hear as much of what they have to say as I can. But when it hits the fan we try to take them together inside."

Mazur and the other patrolman, Dumphy, nodded. Detective Salmons from Homicide just listened.

Proffitt turned to Smith. "Building layout," he said. "Is there a second way up to your apartment, and where is the back door to the building itself?"

King Smith's attitude to events of the evening had been transformed by the prospect of being centrally involved in a police operation. He was now as direct and positive and helpful as he had previously been obstructive. He was eager to provide Proffitt with information. In addition to his clothing and cane, he gave Proffitt suggestions about how to walk to make the best impersonation. "I ran some track in high school," Smith said. "Until I got this leg injury and . . ."

Adele felt out of place, that she was present at the briefing only because she'd come to headquarters in Proffitt's car. Her own was still at the restaurant. When the meeting broke up, however, she did not want to be left behind. She would not feel comfortable not knowing what had happened.

"When things are over, you and Smith will be brought out," Proffitt said.

"I'd rather come now."

"I don't have the time to argue with you, ma'am."

"I'll stay in a car and keep out of the way."

"No," Proffitt said.

"You don't have any choice, Homer. If you don't take

me, I'll come by taxi. At least this way you'll know exactly where I am."

Proffitt felt critical time ebbing away. "Suit your own damn self," he said.

Adele rode with Detective Salmons.

As soon as the operation's three unmarked vehicles had assembled around the corner from Smith's building, Proffitt got things moving.

The patrolmen, Dumphy and Mazur, left their car and went up the alley to enter the building from the back. Proffitt guessed it would take them as many as ten minutes to get inside without attracting attention, but they radioed they were in place in less than five.

Proffitt then began his walk "home."

As he turned the corner on the sidewalk that passed in front of Smith's house, Salmons, with Adele in the passenger seat, drove past him, pulled up short of the house and parked.

Using the cane as Smith had suggested, Proffitt did not hurry.

After a minute he said, over the radio, "I'm coming up to the green BMW under the streetlight short of the house. There's a couple in it necking. Salmons, you and the lady better do the same or look like you're having an argument or something. They will have seen your car pull up and nobody get out. You can't just sit there."

Salmons turned to Adele. He said, "I know which way I'd rather go, Miss."

"Come here, big boy," Adele said.

Proffitt proceeded into the house unmolested.

Dumphy and Mazur met him in the shadows by the stairs inside. Whispering, Proffitt asked, "Anything?"

"No."

"No."

Somewhere nearby they could hear a television. It reminded Proffitt that people other than Smith lived in the building.

Proffitt opened his mouth to speak, but then looked up and blinked a couple of times. Something had occurred to him.

Dumphy and Mazur looked at each other.

Proffitt spoke to his microphone. "Shit! I don't like that courting couple. Salmons, keep an eye on them. If they get out of the car, take them and have the lady honk your horn."

Then to Dumphy and Mazur he nodded. One after the other they walked up the stairs.

The patrolmen tried to synchonize their steps with Proffitt's so as to make it sound like only one person was ascending

On the second-floor landing a door opened a crack as the policemen walked past in unison. A moment later a tiny old man stepped out into the hall and looked up as the three men began to mount the stairs to the top.

Mazur waved and smiled.

The old man immediately retreated into his apartment.

When they reached the top landing, Proffitt took out Smith's keys. He gestured to the others to step to either side. He was just Smith, coming home, expecting nothing unusual. Dumphy and Mazur drew their weapons.

Proffitt pointed to the opposite door, to remind them of the possibility that someone was waiting in the other apartment.

Then he unlocked Smith's door, pushed it open and walked in.

Nothing happened.

He turned on the light.

No one.

The room did not look, superficially, as if it had been searched.

He looked into the apartment's two other rooms.

They were empty.

Proffitt turned to the open doorway, but it was obvious there had been no response to the entry from across the hall. He stepped onto the landing and nodded to the apartment across from Smith's. Quietly he made his way to Donna East's door and tried the knob.

The door swung open.

Nothing happened.

Proffitt went in first.

There was no one there.

"Both apartments are clear," Proffitt said to Salmons. "I'm going to send one of these guys downstairs, Salmons. When he gets there I want the two of you to check out the couple in the car."

"I'll go," Mazur said.

Dumphy turned on the light in Donna East's living room.

When the second light went on upstairs, the necking couple's car came alive. Engine on, lights.

"Shit," Salmons said. There was obviously no time to wait for the other patrolman to come down to help. Salmons thought about whether to get out and try to stop the car on foot.

By the time he failed to decide, the BMW was past them.

"Shit!" Salmons said again. He started his engine and he and Adele took off after it.

The couple was still in sight when Salmons got to the corner and turned after them. Without making a spectacle of himself he gained some ground, and within three blocks the BMW pulled to a stop at a busy intersection, 38th Street.

"Just let me get the plates," Salmons said. "Just let me get the plates."

They pulled up behind the car just as it turned right through a small gap in traffic. The man and the woman in the car were distinct in silhouette. The woman sat close to her door.

They got the plates.

When Adele and Salmons returned to King Smith's building, Proffitt, Dumphy and Mazur were standing on the sidewalk with King Smith and the uniformed officer who had brought him.

Salmons parked across the street. "I think," Salmons said, "that the covert part of this operation is at an end."

He and Adele got out of the car, but before they crossed the street Salmons said, "You did real good, miss."

"Thanks."

"I enjoyed the pretend making-out in the car, too. It flashed me back to when the wife and I were young. I tell you, first time I get the chance I'm going to take her out parking again." He chuckled as they crossed the street. "I tell you, she ain't never going to know what hit her."

"I'm glad *someone* had a good time," Proffitt said sourly to Salmons.

"Sorry," Salmons said.

"I assume that since you and the BMW were gone when we came down that they took off and you followed them."

"That's right," Salmons said. "As soon as the second light came on upstairs, they flew and so did we. But we lost them after they turned off 38th Street north on Meridian. They made the tail end of a light and we were several cars back. We waited for the traffic and screamed up Meridian, but we never picked them up again."

"Did you put out a call?"

"No. I didn't know what kind of call you would want put out. But we got the license plate number."

"Give it to me," Proffitt said tiredly. He led Salmons away to the closest police car.

King Smith approached Adele. He was upset. She asked what was wrong.

"They took things of mine," he said.

"Someone was in your room?"

"They were in there. Sergeant Proffitt had me come up to check. And they took my notes!"

"What notes?" she asked.

"The notes about Donna, when she came and talked to me."

Adele saw that Smith was near tears. "Don't forget," she said, "that I have a photocopy of them."

Smith froze for a moment. "Oh yeah!" he said.

Proffitt turned to the group. "Time to go," he said. He then turned to Salmons and Adele. "Next time," he said sarcastically, "it would be nice if the experts on such things would point out that normal cuddling couples don't park under streetlights." He shook his head. "They were there so they could get a good look at people walking past. So *she* could get a good look at me."

"She?" Adele repeated, catching up with Proffitt's train of thought.

"I reckon the woman in the car was Donna East. Brought here to point Mr. Smith out." He clenched his teeth. "She's sitting in a car and I walk right by her and I fucking miss her. Ma'am."

28

ADELE rode back to headquarters with Salmons.

Proffitt drove alone.

Once there he released Salmons and the two patrolmen and then took Adele to a quiet part of the squad room. "I'm sorry to have been so irritable with you," he said.

"It was disappointing for you to get so close but not have it work out right," Adele said. "And I shouldn't have insisted on coming along when you didn't want me there. It was unprofessional of me."

"I was afraid you would get hurt," Proffitt said. "Ah, well." He lifted his eyebrows to suggest some irony at his own expense, and said, "I did not intend this to be an entirely professional evening. Looks like none of my little plans and speculations worked out quite the way I hoped."

"You've certainly given me an evening to remember," Adele said. "My dinner dates don't normally end up in impromptu police operations."

"Via Brian Wampler and his wife. Now there's an advertisement for marriage."

Thinking of her own motivations and preoccupations,

189

Adele said, "I find myself feeling very involved with Donna East. I didn't want not to be present if you found something out."

"Well, I wanted to say sorry, ma'am."

"What happens now, Homer?"

"I go find out what Communications has on the BMW." He rose. "Coming with me?"

At Communications Proffitt picked up a sheet of paper that had been set aside for him with ownership details on the BMW. With Adele looking over his shoulder he began to read it, but as he did so a Communications officer turned from his console and said, "That's gone on the stolen list."

Proffitt looked up.

"You want it?"

"Sure do," Proffitt said.

"It just came in. The owner only discovered it was gone about half an hour ago."

Proffitt blinked, thinking. Then he said, "All right. Give me a hard copy."

Proffitt and Adele waited through the high-speed whine of the printer as details of the stolen vehicle report were transferred to paper. He added the second sheet to the one he already held and led Adele into the corridor.

"I'm not looking forward to the next few minutes, ma'am."

"No?"

"I've got to see Graniela now. Make a verbal report."

"What are you going to say?"

"I intend to stress the positive."

Adele's face indicated that she was unsure what that might be.

"Somebody *did* go into Smith's apartment. Those notes on Donna East were taken."

"It wasn't you who picked them up, then?"

"You thought I had? To make my case look better?"

Adele shrugged.

"I seem to have confused you about what kind of corners I'll cut to get a result. I may take a risk or two to make things happen faster, but I would *never* invent a fact."

"My turn to apologize," Adele said. "I'm sorry."

"Somebody took those notes, ma'am. And that had to be as a result of Donna East being caught making a telephone call."

Adele nodded.

"And there's also the BMW."

"Will Smith be safe in his apartment tonight?" she said.

"I'd have thought so. They know he got help. That's why they ran. They'll assume it was police."

Adele nodded again.

"I wish I could say the same for Miss Donna East."

Adele said, "Oh, God. How awful."

"Which is what I am about to say to Captain Graniela. I will say, 'Sir, think about what that poor woman is likely being put through at this very moment.' "

"You sound as if Graniela won't agree."

"It kind of depends what mood he's in. He might decide that the car was just a coincidence, that the people in it were under a streetlight so they could find their zippers easier, and when we all showed up it made them nervous."

Adele frowned.

"You don't look like you buy that scenario, ma'am."

"You're the policeman, but if I were going to steal a car to get a little privacy I'd take it out in the country."

"What you say makes a lot of sense, to me. Can I call you in as an expert on joyriding?"

"I do have a friend who occasionally 'borrowed' motor vehicles in his younger days. He did it with a friend who later became a policeman."

"I'm not sure I approve of the company you keep."

"It's all right. I almost never see the policeman."

Proffitt smiled for the first time in hours. Then he said, "Have you noticed that I am delaying going to see Graniela?"

"Yes," she said.

"I wish I had clear in my head what I think about it all." He gave his head one sharp shake. Then, "Look here." He pointed to the stolen car report.

"Where?"

"It says that the owner, Mr. Byron Bradberry, lives on North Meridian Street. What do you think about that?"

"It's where Salmons and I lost it."

"Yes, ma'am. How would your car-thief friend feel about driving a hot car right back up where it was stolen from?"

"He's not a car thief."

"No?" Proffitt said. "Well, maybe you could tell me this, ma'am. Am I right or am I not that there are a lot of big houses up that way on North Meridian Street?"

"You're right."

"Big houses made of brick?"

"What are you trying to say, Homer?"

"Donna East told King Smith she was in a big house made out of brick."

"Yes, but—"

Proffitt held up a hand and Adele stopped talking. He said, "Ma'am, I'm a pretty logical kind of fella. I always have been. Maybe not all that smart, but I have an honest-to-God *passion* for things to fall into their rightful places. And, to be truthful rather than modest, I can't but say I've done pretty well at that kind of thing over the course of my time as a law enforcement officer."

He dropped his eyes to the floor. Adele looked down but saw nothing.

Proffitt continued, saying, "It's never hard to fit pieces

together when you've got them all. That's the logic. But knowing where to look for the pieces, that's more in the area of following your feelings."

"And you have a feeling now?"

"Yes ma'am."

"What is it, Homer?"

"I have the feeling that it would fit pretty good if Miss Donna East made her telephone call to Mr. King Smith from the home of Mr. Byron Bradberry of North Meridian Street."

Adele considered the suggestion.

Proffitt said, "Now, I haven't ever seen that house, but I can just about picture it right now. Made of brick . . ." He smiled at himself and what could easily be called his flight of fancy. "A spread-out kind of house, with telephones on little tables in hallways and thick carpets and everything beige."

Adele said nothing.

"And I can see other things too, ma'am. And they aren't any of them very good for the future of Miss Donna East."

"What do you want to do, Homer?"

"I *want* to get on the radio and get a dozen cars over to the house of Mr. Byron Bradberry and go through it and find Miss Donna East and her little girls. And I also want to do it because I think Mr. Byron Bradberry and his friends are about to dump this so-called stolen car." Another sharp shake of the head. "You take a look at the time of the missing vehicle report, ma'am."

Adele looked.

Proffitt said, "They reported it stolen about twenty minutes after you and Salmons lost it."

"Yes?"

"It would seem to me to fit if these people originally went to Mr. King Smith's apartment in a big hurry after they caught Donna on the telephone. And if they went in the nearest available car, their own. And if when they took off from outside Mr. King Smith's apartment they didn't do anything but drive their car right back home. That's what I think happened."

Proffitt nodded vigorously. He seemed to be working himself up for his imminent interview with Graniela.

"I wouldn't even be sure they had any idea they were being followed. *But* I also think that once they got home they got worried that somebody did notice the car and maybe took the plate number. So they reported it stolen so they could claim the car had nothing to do with them."

Adele waited at Proffitt's desk while he reported to Graniela. She found her feelings divided about Homer Proffitt, wondering if he wasn't just creating dramatic scenes to compensate for the comparative failure of the enterprise at King Smith's.

But she was also unquestionably affected by the passion he evinced and the scenario he had drawn. Ambition-driven he might be, but Proffitt was a dedicated man and an intelligent and inventive one.

While she waited, Adele tried to make two telephone calls. However, both Lucy and Al were out.

As time passed Adele felt increasingly impatient and impotent and inclined to do something.

Proffitt's face showed the interview with Graniela had not gone well.

Before he was close enough for Adele to ask what had been said, he gestured to her to follow him. She did so, and they passed silently to the elevator. He was clearly deep in thought.

Adele said nothing.

They rode to the basement in silence.

They walked the corridor to Proffitt's car in silence.

After getting in, they sat for a moment in silence.

Then Proffitt said, "He was quite reasonable, in a way."

She waited for the *but*.

"But he sure wouldn't give me no more rope to wrap around my poor 'ol country neck, ma'am, and I sure do want it."

Adele waited.

"Captain Graniela says drop it. He says there is no evidence of a connection between the BMW and Donna East and no justification for sending the calvary to Byron Bradberry's. He says I had my shot. He says it didn't exactly miss but it didn't hit anything, either. He says that's it. Quit until there's a better reason to believe that Donna East has come to grief."

"What are you going to do, Homer?"

"I am seriously considering a course of action that could well have me back in Evansville this weekend, permanently."

"Resignation?"

"What?" he asked. Then he laughed. "No, no ma'am. Much worse than that."

"Oh."

"Sounds pretty drastic, doesn't it?" He started the car.

"What are you planning to do?"

"I'm going to go to Mr. Byron Bradberry's by myself and see if I can sort something out."

"Even though Graniela has told you not to."

"That's right." He turned to her, smiling. "I will happily drop you off where you can pick up your car, ma'am. Or if you want to make it a full and complete evening, you can come along and witness the full and complete end of the police career of Homer Proffitt, the chief that never was."

29

THE Bradberry house on North Meridian was, as Proffitt
had predicted, a sprawling brick mansion with a lot of
land. Built in the twenties and canopied at the front by
nineteenth-century trees, it separated the "them" of the
sidewalk from the "us" of the estate by an iron fence
topped with arrowheads. The metal barrier was broken
only by an open gate to an S-shaped driveway that led in
from the street. The drive came in on the north side,
snaked past the front of the house and tailed behind on
the south, presumably leading to garages.

At the entrance to the driveway Proffitt said, "I'd hoped
I could take a walk around the place before going up to
introduce myself, but I wonder if that's the right way to
go about things here."

He wasn't asking for comment. He was thinking out
loud, a courtesy to keep Adele in touch with his
plans.

"No," he said, "if they're up to things, they're going
to be aware of what happens outside. Rich people likely
have dogs or cameras. Getting caught on the prowl would
undercut my position. We'll go in face first."

Proffitt drove the car up the drive. He passed the door

and continued on the driveway to its turn toward the back of the house. But Proffitt didn't follow the asphalt. He left his vehicle sprawled across the bend, blocking it.

They got out and went to the front door.

Proffitt rang the doorbell. Adele was nervous as she waited. Her heart thumped and her mouth went dry and she wondered seriously what she was doing there.

"Won't be long now, ma'am," Proffitt said. He rang the bell again.

Almost immediately, the door opened to the length of a restraining chain. A tall, thin, gray-haired man in his sixties was visible through the gap. "Yes?" he asked.

Proffitt opened a wallet and displayed his shield. He said, "I'm here to see Mr. Bradberry."

The man hesitated. "I am Major Bradberry," he said.

"It's about the stolen car, Major."

"Ah, the car," he said. He thought. "Has it been found?"

"No," Proffitt said.

"What is it about the car, then?"

"I want to get information about it from you, sir."

"But I explained the details to a policeman not long ago."

"That was a patrolman, right? A guy in uniform?"

"He was in uniform, yes."

Proffitt smiled. "Well, sir, it's a quiet night, so we're pulling out the big guns for you. I'm from Quad I detective branch. The theory is that I'm going to have a better chance of getting the car back for you than if we just leave it to routine procedures."

"I see," Major Bradberry said. It was not entirely apparent whether he saw or not.

"Look," Proffitt asked easily, "are you going to let us in or do we freeze our buns here on the doorstep all night?" ·

Major Bradberry considered. Then he closed the door to undo the chain.

"*Major* Bradberry?" Proffitt said guardedly to Adele. "What the hell kind of setup is this?"

The door opened. Major Bradberry stepped back. Proffitt and Adele walked in.

The hall carpets were beige.

"Is there somewhere we can sit down and be a little comfortable while I get the facts?" Proffitt asked.

"The library I think," Bradberry said. He about-faced and set off down the wide hallway.

His visitors followed.

As Bradberry approached an open doorway, he moved to it, but he only stopped and leaned in. "More police, dear," he said. He continued farther down the hall.

As she passed the open door, Adele saw a woman sitting alone at a large, oval dining table. The woman was shuffling a pack of cards. She seemed, from a glance, to be fiftyish. She didn't look up.

Major Bradberry's library was remarkably bare of books. Half a dozen large dark volumes with no names on the spines were tucked up tightly by a bookend on the bottom shelf of an otherwise empty bookcase.

The center of the room was dominated by a large wooden desk, heavy, dark and rough. Its top was completely bare, but the surface was not polished or even smooth. Small flecks of bare wood were visible here and there as if it had been picked at occasionally over many semesters by small children.

A window with venetian blinds looked over the southern, driveway side of the house. Though the blinds were open, no outside features were visible.

Major Bradberry sat behind his desk. Proffitt and Adele were waved to choose between a small couch and two hardbacked chairs. They took the chairs and Proffitt moved his ostentatiously to the front of the desk and opened a notebook on the surface.

Major Bradberry watched without expression.

"Which service were you in, Major?" Proffitt asked.

"The Army," Bradberry said.

"Great."

"The British Army."

"Are you English?"

"I am British," Bradberry said.

"Now you mention it, I can hear something in your voice. Not the way you pronounce words so much as a kind of clipped rhythm as you say them. How long you been living here?"

"Thirty-one years. My wife inherited the use of this house from her mother's brother."

"Nice place."

Major Bradberry touched a hand to his forehead, held it there for a moment and then placed it on the desktop. "Can we get on about the car, please?"

Though balked in his apparently casual attempt to get the family background, Proffitt nodded and said, "Of course."

He went through the basic details. When had the car been missed, from where, when reported . . .

Major Bradberry said that he and his wife found the car was gone when they left the house to drive to see a film.

"Kind of late to go off to the movies, wasn't it?" Proffitt suggested.

"My wife and I do not retire early," Bradberry said.

"Was that your wife we passed on the way here?"

"Yes."

"Any kids?"

"We have one son."

"Does he live here?"

"He does." Major Bradberry squinted at Proffitt, almost his first facial expression. "Is that relevant to the matter at hand?"

"Well, I thought I might have a word with anybody else who was around the house tonight. Maybe somebody saw something, heard something. What with the missing vehicle having been stolen right off the premises here."

"No one saw anything," Bradberry said. "I've spoken to them all."

"Who would 'they all' be?"

"My wife and my son."

"Nobody else?"

"No."

"Isn't it a pretty big place to run by yourselves?"

"No one lives here except ourselves."

"Do you mind if I ask you a sort of personal question?"

Bradberry hesitated. "I think I do mind," he said.

Undeterred, Proffitt said, "It was only whether you folks are a little short of cash these days."

Bradberry said nothing.

"A lot of people in this kind of house along North Meridian have servants."

"We have a cleaner. She comes in on Tuesdays."

"I meant a lot of people have live-in staff."

"Not us."

"Tough to get good help, huh?"

Bradberry did not respond.

Proffitt turned to his notebook and said, "I don't know if the uniformed officer mentioned it, Major, but we had a sighting of your car."

After a pause, Bradberry said, "Did you indeed?"

"Yes. It was seen very close to the time you reported it stolen."

"But the car hasn't been recovered?"

"No. But the funny thing is that the car was spotted very close to here. Coming from the direction of town up North Meridian Street."

"Oh."

"That's strange, isn't it? It is seen at a point some way from this house, and instead of going farther away it goes toward it."

The major did not respond.

"Well, sometimes, you know, members of a family take a car and don't tell each other and people think it's been stolen."

"That is not the case in this instance."

"Of course not. But there are other times," Proffitt said, "thieves take a car and finish what they want to do with it, and then bring it back to the place that they stole it from."

"I see."

"You get all kinds of car thief these days. Some of them treat the cars quite well and"—a glance at Adele—"know some real respectable people."

Major Bradberry said nothing in the pause Proffitt offered.

Proffitt asked, "Is there a back way into this place? I mean for a car?"

"There is a connection to an alley at the back of the property."

"What I was thinking was, given how this is a big place and there are only the three of you here and there is a back entrance as well as the front one, what I wondered was whether you mind if I take a little look around. You never know. Your car might be right outside somewhere and you wouldn't even know it."

Major Bradberry was beginning to speak when outside the library window a car door closed.

Proffitt blinked. Then he jumped out of his chair and ran to the window.

A motor started.

Proffitt ran from the room.

30

As Proffitt disappeared, Major Bradberry rose from his chair behind the desk. He faced Adele, open-mouthed.

Adele could think of nothing to say.

"What an extraordinary thing to do," Bradberry said at last.

"Yes," Adele agreed.

There was no advance on that.

Adele was engulfed in a wave of uncomfortableness. She rose from her seat. "I do assure you," she said, "that Detective Sergeant Proffitt is a very capable police officer."

For the first time Major Bradberry was speaking other than in direct answer to a question. He said, "I never cease to wonder at the behavior of people in this country."

Suddenly Adele felt the sadness in the man. She asked, "Are you not happy here?"

"Life is very complicated," he said. "Very, very, very, very complicated." He paused. The sojourn into himself was over. He sat down and said, "Shouldn't you be trying to find your colleague?"

"Of course," Adele said. She took a step toward the

door, but then went back to collect Proffitt's notebook from the desktop.

Major Bradberry remained at his desk. He put a hand to his forehead again.

Adele left the room.

Proffitt's car was gone from the front of the house.

Adele stood in the open front door, continuing in her uncomfortable and uncertain frame of mind. What was she supposed to do? Wait until he got back? Leave on foot? Look around outside?

As she stood in the doorway, Adele grew angry. In one sense she'd been lured into a complex situation and then left in a false position by a man she hardly knew.

Then the focus of the anger passed to herself. She was adult: She had volunteered, even been eager. And she had also temporarily forgotten that it was Donna East she was there for.

Adele turned back into the house.

In the dining room the woman was still playing cards. Without looking up she said, "Come in, my dear."

Adele entered.

"I am Lavinia Bradberry."

"Adele Buffington."

"Sit down."

Adele pulled out one of the chairs from the table and turned it to face Mrs. Bradberry's.

"That's right, dear," the woman said, "make yourself all comfy."

"You are Major Bradberry's wife?" Adele asked.

"It would be a pretty rum situation if I weren't," the woman said. Then she sighed. "Such is my fate." The woman spoke with accent similar to her husband's.

Adele didn't know what she should be talking about with Mrs. Bradberry. So she spoke what first came to mind, the same question she'd asked the major. "Are . . . are you not happy over here?"

"We don't have much choice. This is where the house is."

"Houses can be sold."

"Not this one, honey!" This was said more Americanly; a joke?

Mrs. Bradberry looked at Adele for the first time. The look was long and assessing. She sighed again and turned back to the cards. "It's not ours, dear. It was left to our son, Anthony, although my husband and I are free to live here for as long as we remain alive."

"Have you only the one child?"

"Oh yes," Mrs. Bradberry said, as if the idea of her having more than one child was utterly unthinkable.

The women sat in silence as Mrs. Bradberry continued to play cards. After a minute she asked, "Am I wrong, or did the person you arrived with not run out the front door and drive away?"

"I think he did, yes."

"Did the major displease him *so* much?" The question was both one of great fatigue and mild humor.

"A car started outside. Detective Sergeant Proffitt thought it might have something to do with the stolen car."

"Ah, the stolen car," Mrs. Bradberry said, without much interest.

"I gather that your son still lives with you."

"We live with him," she corrected immediately.

"Yes. I meant, often . . . well, children don't often live together with their parents when they are grown up."

"I suppose Anthony is grown up," Mrs. Bradberry said laconically. "At thirty-three I suppose he is."

"What does he do?" Adele asked.

"For a living, you mean?"

"Yes."

"That I couldn't tell you."

"Oh."

"We don't talk much to Anthony. Or he to us."

"I see."

"He does *something*, I know that. He always has more money than his rather outdated trust fund provides for him. But he isn't trained for anything, and whatever it is that he does, I don't think it's a regular job."

Mrs. Bradberry turned over a card.

"He never liked school here much," she said. "He's never been quite—what do they say these days? Not quite macho enough to feel comfortable in the rah-rah belt."

"What did you do before this inheritance happened?"

"Oh, Nigel was in the Army. Doing rather well, too. At least I think he was."

"You could have stayed there."

"We would have lost this place. One of the conditions, you see."

"But if you're not happy . . ."

"*Happy? Happy?* Why is the ultimate standard always *happy* these days?"

Adele didn't answer, and it didn't seem to her that she was expected to. Lavinia Bradberry said, "At the time, we thought we were doing the best for the child."

Adele began to speak, then stopped.

"Is something wrong, my dear?"

"On the vehicle ownership report we got down at headquarters, it said that the owner of the car was a Byron Bradberry."

"Yes."

"But if your husband's first name is Nigel, and your son's is Anthony . . . ?"

"Anthony's first name is Byron."

"Oh."

"We were rather 'into' poetry about the time that he came along."

"I see."

"We've entirely lost interest now."

"Oh."

"All these dreadful new buildings," she said suddenly. "And no concern at all about what goes on in them."

Adele was thinking about what this might mean when Major Bradberry appeared at the door.

"Ah," he said. "You're being looked after, then."

"Yes," Adele said. She wondered suddenly if she shouldn't be doing something other than sitting talking to dispirited people who had transplanted themselves to a cultural soil that was too thin for them.

"Your colleague doesn't seem to have come back," the major said.

"No."

"Extraordinary thing to do," Major Bradberry said. "Did you know, Lavinia, he just jumped up and ran out, like . . . like . . . like I don't know what. Extraordinary."

"Yes, dear, I know."

Adele said, "I think he thought he had to act quickly or he would miss his chance."

"Without a thought for what he left behind," Major Bradberry said. "American philosophy in a nutshell."

"I don't know about that," Adele said.

"I suppose I could call a taxi for you."

"Perhaps that might be best."

"Unless I could tempt you to join me in a Scotch whisky."

"Don't use the poor girl as an excuse, Nigel. She's on duty."

"Major, Mrs. Bradberry," Adele said impulsively, "since I'm already here, do you mind if I have a look around?"

31

As Adele left the dining room, Major Bradberry was pouring drinks for himself and his wife. On the beige central corridor, Adele turned toward the depths of the house.

Walking slowly, she passed the library and came to the end of the hall. Here the way split, giving her the choice of turning to the right or the left along a tiled hallway or of continuing straight ahead through ornately carved, dark wooden double doors.

Adele tried the handle and both doors opened. She entered a wide room that made the top of a T with the hallway. In the middle, running almost the entire length, was a table. The floor of the room was polished wood. She saw immediately two kinds of extravagant use for the space: banquets and balls!

It was the idea of a ball that took her imagination. Too many dishes to wash after a banquet.

But the dust on the table and on the floor suggested that the householders here made no use of the room, extravagant or otherwise.

Adele circled the table to the opposite wall, which was

filled by drapes. She hunted for and found where they met and looked behind. Floor-to-ceiling windows.

What a wonderful room.

Outside the banquet-ball hall was a courtyard.

On the right, southern, side of the open area muted lights showed through two windows. It wasn't clear to Adele whether these rooms were lit or whether the lights shone from deeper inside. Either way, they gave just enough illumination across the courtyard to show that the house had back wings running down each side of the central space.

Adele turned away from the window wall. She continued around the table, making tracks on the floor, and left the room by the exquisite double doors. She then considered which way to go on the tiled hallway that ran to right and left.

She decided for the direction toward the wing where lights were on.

Drawn toward the light?

This was also the driveway side of the house, where the car Proffitt was chasing had come from.

Adele walked slowly, listening, looking. She heard nothing. Saw nothing animate.

After the hallway turned the corner at the end of the ballroom, the floor suddenly became carpeted again. It was like a boundary line on a map or the way road surfaces sometimes change at a state line. The painted walls gave way to flock wallpaper. The fluorescent ceiling lights became brass wall fittings topped with bottle-shaped glass shades to suggest kerosene lamps. Pictures hung on the walls.

The first picture was a Mondrian print, lines and spaces titled "Boogie Woogie." The second was a reproduction of an untitled British fox-hunting scene.

Then there was a door.

Adele hesitated outside it, but with Proffitt out somewhere chasing "Anthony's" car, and both senior Bradberrys sipping Scotch in the other dining room, she turned the handle.

The door was unlocked.

The room was unlit.

Adele stepped forward, located a switch on the wall, and turned the light on.

She found she had entered a small bedroom. A three-quarters bed was made up on the wall opposite her. There was a table beside it with a telephone. Surfaces were clear, and nothing personal or individual was in evidence.

A guest room?

She went to the telephone. She lifted the receiver by the two ends, so as not to disturb any fingerprints on the middle.

She heard a dial tone.

She wondered whether she should call someone.

To say what?

She replaced the telephone and looked again around the room.

There was a closet. She hesitated, but again overcame her sense of unease and opened the door.

It was empty, except for seven coat hangers.

Adele closed the closet, turned off the light and returned to the hall. She closed the room door.

The next picture was a large Ingres nude.

Followed by another door. The opposite side.

Looking up and down the hallway first, Adele entered again.

Again the light was off, but the illumination from the hallway showed immediately that this was not a bedroom.

She found the switch. Turning the light on lit a large table filled with electric trains, tracks, villages, geographical features. A miniature world.

Her first impulse was to run her finger over the surface edge, and she did so.

Not dusty, this one.

At the end of the room was a workbench, and it bore a number of small tools and some electric gauges.

Also a telephone.

She went to the phone and picked up the receiver as she had with the last one. She heard a dial tone, and put it back.

Next to the bench there was a closet door.

Inside, a massive collection of children's board games was neatly shelved.

Adele returned to the trains and went to the controls. She was tempted to throw a switch, to see if she could bring it to life. She touched the transformer. It was cold. But instead of following her impulse, she left the room.

The Bradberrys thought she was a police officer, but that wouldn't be excuse enough to risk breaking something.

The next picture was a photograph of a Greek jar.

Another door.

Other side.

With less hesitation than before she opened it and turned on the light.

She found herself facing six naked women.

Shocked not to be alone, Adele made an audible sound.

The women said nothing.

They were all blondes. Each had bright blue eyes, dramatic, protuberant breasts and prominent pudenda. Each stood on slightly bowed legs.

Adele relaxed again.

The women were identical, motionless. And plastic.

Adele stepped into the room.

On the floor behind the door was an orgy of plastic flesh, perhaps another dozen "women." They lay in an untidy and awkward mound, piled against the wall. There seemed some variation among the stacked inflatables, with a range of hair colors and other design differences.

Near the bottom of the pile, at the leg end, Adele saw a shoe. The shoe was real and human, compared to the plastic "people."

The room had another telephone. Adele went to it and lifted the receiver as before. She poised a finger to punch a number.

But this time there was no dial tone.

She put the receiver down again. She was breathing hard.

She followed the the wire extending from the back of the phone. She found its ripped-out end.

Next to the phone table was a closet door.

Before turning to leave the room, she stepped to the door and opened it.

The closet was empty.

She felt a wave of sadness.

Behind her a man said, "I see you've discovered my little secret."

32

ADELE jerked around toward the voice.

In the doorway stood a slightly built man wearing only a red towel wrapped around his waist. He was in his early thirties, five eightish, and he had sandy hair and soft facial features.

He also held a small automatic pistol.

His grip on the weapon seemed relaxed, but it was pointed steadily at the middle of Adele's body.

"My lovely ladies," he said. "They're extremely well made, you know. Not junk that springs a leak unless you're 'nice' to them."

Adele said—could say—nothing.

"They have all the essential features. Some little extras, too." The man's face took on an artificially friendly smile. "Notice the erect nipples."

Adele didn't move.

The man's smile inverted to a sudden frown. "Go on. Look!"

Adele glanced at the dolls. When she returned to the man the "smile" was back in place.

"You nearly scared me to death," Adele said. Then she regretted her choice of words.

"I'm sorry if I distressed you," the man said. "Perhaps I should have knocked." In case she had missed the sarcasm, he added, "Knocked and asked permission to enter a room in my own house."

Adele's hands gripped her forearms. Her mouth was dry. She said, "I didn't think anybody was here."

"Obviously."

"I mean, I was told—well, almost told . . ." Her voice faded as she failed, in her nervousness, to remember exactly what she had been told.

"Are you a burglar?" the man asked. The tone was aggressive.

"I came to the house with Detective Sergeant Proffitt," Adele said. In case *he* missed the point: "Of the police."

The man considered this.

"Detective Proffitt is out investigating the theft of a car from these premises earlier in the evening."

"Is he, now?"

"Major and Mrs. Bradberry gave me permission to look around the house while I wait for Detective Proffitt to return."

This irritated the man. "The house is not theirs to give permissions in," he said.

"Is it . . . Are you the owner, Byron Anthony Bradberry?"

Her knowledge of his full name impressed him more than the verbal invocation of the police had. "I am," he said.

"Oh." Adele felt weak, and was unable to build on her moment of advantage. Proffitt's assumption, she was sure, was that the son had driven away in the car he was chasing. Her own impulse to explore had certainly been based on that assumption.

"What are you searching for?" Bradberry asked.

"I was just looking around," she said. Try to gather some initiative, push this police connection. "I was checking to see whether anything was amiss."

"All part of the police service?"

Be careful. "It's better to be careful than careless."

"I hate self-righteous platitudes," Bradberry said. Then, "Perhaps you can tell me exactly how picking up telephone receivers furthers a stolen car investigation?"

Adele was surprised. "Uh . . ."

"In *my* room I have a switchboard that shows when the telephones in *my* house are being used. For all *I* know you were planning to use my telephones to make personal calls. Long distance. International."

"I didn't use the phones. I just checked that they were working."

"Why?"

Adele found the question unanswerable. Instead she said, "I don't know whether you know, but the telephone in this room is faulty."

"Why were you testing the telephones?" Insistent.

Adele shook her head. "Honestly," she said, "I don't know. It just seemed something to do."

The man did not seem content with this response to his question.

"Would you mind putting that gun down, Mr. Bradberry?" Adele said.

"I think I would mind."

"It makes me uncomfortable."

"You make me uncomfortable," he said.

"There's no reason why I should," she said.

"I think I'll be the judge of that," he said.

"I certainly didn't mean to disturb you," Adele said. "If you wish to confirm with your parents that I was wandering around with their authorization, please do so. If you wish me to leave, I'll go. I'm not looking for anything specific here. I'm not going to find a stolen car in one of these rooms, now am I? Basically I am just passing time until Detective Proffitt returns, but if you prefer that I do it elsewhere, I will."

"I think," Bradberry said, "that I would like to see your identification."

"I don't have it on me," Adele said.

"That sounds extremely suspicious."

"I left my handbag in Detective Proffitt's car. Since he's taken the car, I am without ID."

Byron Bradberry stared at her.

"Look, just come with—"

"Assume the position," Bradberry said.

"What?"

"Assume the position!"

"You mean—"

"I mean lean against the wall and spread your legs."

"I don't think—"

He raised the gun and shouted, "Do it, damn you!"

Adele did it.

Her position was not to Bradberry's satisfaction. He kicked at her feet to move them so far back that it was all she could do to keep from falling.

Then Bradberry patted her all over with his free hand. he did it slowly and thoroughly. Giving himself a little treat.

Adele bore it in silence. Saying anything, resisting, would give him more pleasure.

When Bradberry was finished, he stepped back and said, "All right."

Awkwardly, Adele stood up and moved away from the wall. She turned to him to find that he was smiling again, this time broadly.

Bradberry said, "All cops carry guns. You aren't carrying a gun."

"I told you, my handbag is in—"

He lifted a hand. "Are you or are you not a cop?"

"I never said I was."

"I realize that," Bradberry said, barely able to contain the glee of his discovery. "So now that we have ascertained what you are not, why don't you tell me what you are."

"I am a social worker."

His face wrinkled. He thought. He asked, "What is a social worker doing here?"

"I came with Detective Sergeant Proffitt."

"So you keep telling me, lady, but what you say simply doesn't make much sense. I don't like puzzles and teases." Bradberry's face reddened. He moved his hands with emphasis. The gun swung back and forth.

Adele was suddenly very frightened.

Bradberry continued, clearly agitated, "Even if you were a cop, you didn't have *any* excuse to go prowling around the house. And as a social worker it's incomprehensible!"

"I told you, I got permission from your parents."

"But *why* did you ask for that particular permission?" The voice rose in tone. "What do you think you are looking for? You better tell me." He raised the gun. He was nearly screaming. "You better tell me now, because if you don't, you're dead meat!"

Adele was breathing so quickly that she could hardly speak. With as much force and conviction as she could muster, she said, "To tell you the truth, your parents made me uncomfortable. I was there in the dining room with them, and I thought if I asked to look around the house it would be a way of not having to spend the time waiting with them."

Bradberry stared at her again.

"I was just passing the time till Proffitt gets back. They thought I was a police officer, too."

She felt that his not speaking was hopeful, that perhaps she had struck a chord in him about his parents.

"Ask them, for God's sake," she said.

"I don't ask them things," Bradberry said. "I tell them things, and they do them."

He breathed heavily, loudly. He stared at her.

Adele couldn't think of anything more to say that might help. She took a step toward the door.

Bradberry decided.

He shook his head.

"You are going nowhere," he said. *"Nowhere!"* He raised the gun.

She leaned back.

He said, "Take off—"

Bradberry was interrupted by a voice calling him from outside the room.

33

THE voice was male and a little unsteady. "Anthony? Anthony?" The door handle turned.

Bradberry blocked the door with his foot.

"Son? You're in there, I can hear you. There's something I want to say to you."

Bradberry exhaled furiously. Then in a sudden movement he pulled the door open and faced his father.

"Ah, there you are."

"You know that you are not allowed back here."

"It's just that there is a policewoman—"

Adele pushed herself into the doorway. Bradberry blocked her departure, but she was visible.

"Oh, there you are!" Major Bradberry stood in the hallway before them, holding his glass with both hands. "I see you've met." He peered into the room. "Oh, he's showing you his women." Major Bradberry looked at Adele. He looked at the "women." He looked back to Adele. "Extraordinary," he said.

"I was just coming to talk to you," Adele said.

The major said, "Son, your mother thought you would want to be told someone was in the house. We tried to get through on the telephone but there was no answer. Maybe they're broken or something."

"Get the fuck out of here!" Bradberry said.

"All right! All right!" Major Bradberry took one hand away from the glass and waved it. "Just thought you would want to know." He addressed Adele. "Something you wanted to say to me, was there?"

"Yes."

"I'll wait for you at the end of the hall, young woman."

"Thank you," Adele said, with feeling.

Major Bradberry did an uneasy right turn and made his way slowly back toward the front of the house.

Anthony continued to bar Adele's way out.

"Detective Proffitt will be back soon," Adele said. "And remember, I would be missed. He—they—would come looking for me."

Bradberry did not respond.

A sudden impulse. "And there is no reason for me to tell anybody about your, your . . ." She pointed to the standing dolls.

"What about them?"

"That's what you're so edgy about, isn't it? I mean, it's not nice to find someone in your house unexpectedly, but that's not enough to make you wave a gun and threaten me."

"I didn't threaten you," Bradberry said.

Adele didn't argue the point. She said, "So, are these . . . things illegal? It's the only reason I can think of that could make you so upset about my being here."

Bradberry lowered the gun.

Adele exhaled with relief, so loudly she thought the sound might disturb him again.

"I don't sell them, you know," he said.

"No?"

"I just like them around."

"Oh."

"I play strip poker with them."

"Oh," Adele said.

There was a pause. Adele took a step toward the arms that blocked her way through the door. "I think I'd better get back out to the front of the house now," she said. "Detective Proffitt may have returned already."

After a moment in which their faces were only a couple of inches apart, Bradberry dropped his arm and retreated.

But as she moved past him, he took hold of her shoulder and held it hard. He looked at her carefully. Adele couldn't see where the gun was.

Bradberry said, "You've got quite a nice body. Would you like to play poker with me sometime?"

Adele glanced back at the naked dolls. "You're too good a card player for me, Mr. Bradberry."

He hesitated. He dropped his hold on her. "Yeah," he said, "I guess I am."

She stepped clear of him into the corridor.

Bradberry followed her. He pulled the red towel away from his waist.

"I was taking a shower," he said. "I was dirty. But I'm clean now. See?"

As Adele turned the corner at the end of the hall, she felt her first bit of relief.

She didn't slow down. She didn't greet Major Bradberry, who was refilling his glass from a leather-covered flask. She continued to the central hallway and headed for the front door.

Neither the bit of relief nor the increasing safety slackened her need to get out of this house.

The chain was on the front door again. As she fought to slide it off she found it difficult to control the movement of her own hands. She worked at the chain for an eternity. She pounded on the door in frustration.

Behind her Major Bradberry stepped into the hall. "You're not leaving us, are you?" he called.

Adele solved the chain. Wrenched at the doorknob. Threw the door open.

Ran.

34

ADELE nearly lost her balance on the steps down to the snaking drive, but once at the bottom she sprinted for the street.

Major Bradberry arrived in the doorway and watched. He drank from his tumbler.

Adele turned left when she reached the sidewalk, heading south, where she knew she would eventually find telephone booths.

The sound from each passing car made her shiver, but she didn't look at any of them or slow down.

After what seemed forever she saw the Tarkington Park tennis courts across the street and then ahead of her phones on the other side of 38th Street.

She was nearly there. At the same time she felt her breath was totally used up.

She stopped and bent over, gasping.

She stood for only a few moments, the urge to move forward overcoming all pain. She began to walk. It was hard at first to keep a straight line, hard to stand straight up.

Then the light at 38th Street seemed to hold her up forever.

On the other side, telephones. A pair.

She thought about what she should say, to make the police do what she needed to have them do.

The lights changed. She crossed the street.

In the first booth the receiver was ripped out.

But the second, thankfully, offered a dial tone. She dialed 911. She asked the emergency operator to connect her to the police, urgently.

"Indianapolis Police Emergency."

Listen to me very carefully," Adele said. "I have just seen a dead body, a woman who has been murdered. You must get patrol cars there immediately so that the murderer does not have time to dispose of the body."

"May I have your name, please?"

"Did you hear what I said?"

"All emergency calls are automatically timed and recorded. I need your name."

Adele gave her name.

"Address."

Adele gave her address. But her anger at the delay grew and made her strong.

"Now," the emergency officer began.

"Connect me to whoever is in charge of Homicide," Adele said.

"If you'll just give me the details of—"

"This is a matter of murder," Adele shouted. "It'll be your ass in a sling if you don't put me through, *now!*"

There was a pause. "Just a moment."

Adele banged at the telephone booth's plastic "glass" with a fist. It popped out of its casing.

A telephone receiver was picked up. "Homicide. Lieutenant Malmberg."

When she finished talking to Malmberg, Adele dialed the operator. "I want to make a collect call," she said, and gave the operator the number.

As it rang, Adele said, "Be there. Be there."

The telephone was answered. "Albert Samson."
The operator said, "I have a collect call from—"
Adele shouted over him, "Albert! Help me!"

Adele waited in the recessed doorway of the drug-
store on the corner.
Cars passed on 38th Street. Cars passed on Meridian.
She listened for sirens, but heard none.
She looked for Al, but he didn't come.
She was tired and angry and her chest hurt from so
much breathing and her legs hurt from too much run-
ning.
Two large young men jogged past her along 38th
Street. They went to the corner and waited for the light.
One glanced back at her. They exchanged words.
The light turned green for them, but instead of cross-
ing Meridian they turned back. They looked around. They
approached Adele.
Adele glared at them.
The taller of the young men asked, "You got a light?"
"No," Adele said.
The shorter of the young men grimaced and said,
"Listen good, lady. This is a gun in my pocket. Give us
your money or we'll be real bad to you."
"Fuck off!" Adele screamed at them. "Just go fuck off!"
The two men looked at each other.
They jogged away.

At last Al's rusty van pulled up and stopped.
He left the motor running, got out and vaulted the
low pedestrian guardrail.
Adele stepped out of the drugstore doorway and
walked toward him.
"Sorry," he said, approaching. "The damn thing
wouldn't start at first."
"Oh, Al!"

"Are you all right?" he asked. "Are you all right?"

"Get me home. Get me home."

Adele rode shaking and hugging herself. Al put his arm around her whenever it could be spared from the driving.

When they arrived, he helped her get out of the van and enter her house.

"I'll put you to bed," Al said.

"The couch," she said. "I'm all right."

"Sure?"

"There will be things to be explained."

He took her to the couch in the living room and sat her down.

"I'm going crazy," she said.

She shivered, and he held her close.

She said, "It was a nightmare over and over." Meaning being subjected to threats and abuse. Meaning that after a lifetime without experiencing personal violence she had been confronted by two—two!—demented, dangerous men—killers—in less than three days.

She laughed suddenly. "And then two muggers, who said they would be bad to me!" She laughed again.

Al had no idea what she was laughing about.

"It's enough to make you think all men should be put down," she said.

She shook her head.

She nodded.

Al sat with her, making contact, trying to warm her.

When finally she was calmer he said, "I'm going to get you a blanket."

He left and came back with a blanket from her bed. He wrapped it around her and left again for the kitchen, where he poured her some rum. He set the glass on the table beside her.

He sat on the floor and rubbed her legs.

"It was the shoe," Adele said. "I saw the shoe, and then I saw everything."

"The shoe?"

"Among all that plastic, the shoe was *real*," she said. "It was worn. It had chewing gum on the sole." She laughed a little, quietly and uneasily.

Then they heard noises at the door.

"What now?" Al said.

They heard the front door open.

The noises moved down the hall and entered the room.

Lucy was first in, followed by a fat young man with bright, rodent eyes. Lucy was saying to the young man, "I told you they might still be up."

Then she said, "Hello, Mother, Al. This is Fritz. He's come to stay the night with me. There's no problem about that, is there?"

35

THE police arrived at the house at 3:00 A.M.

Adele was dozing on the couch, having refused to go to bed. "I need to know what's happened to Homer," she had said.

"I can make a few phone calls."

"They'll be coming here anyway."

And they did.

Al answered the door.

A pallid policeman in an expensive suit identified himself as Detective Lieutenant Malmberg. He asked to speak to Miss or Mrs. Adele Buffington, and Al brought him into the living room.

Adele was sitting up. Her eyes were puffy.

"Mrs. Buffington?"

"I generally prefer *Ms.*," she said.

Malmberg made a note.

"Be quiet, please," Adele said. She spoke wanly. "My daughter is upstairs and I don't want to disturb her."

"I don't plan to shout," Malmberg said, "but I sure need to know just what your connection to that house is, and how the hell you knew there were bodies underneath them goddamn dolls."

"*Bodies?*" Adele asked.

"A woman and two little Mongoloid girls."

"Oh, God!"

Both men watched as the news took a physical toll on Adele. Breathing, eyes, muscle control . . .

After a time she said, "I'll be all right in a minute. Just make me a cup of tea, will you?"

Al went to the kitchen to make some tea.

Malmberg was uneasy, impatient. When they were alone he said, "If you would—"

Adele held up a hand to stop him.

He sighed audibly. He sat back in his chair to wait.

Al brought the tea. Adele blew on it, sipped from it. She said, "How did I know there was a body there?"

"That's right."

"I saw a shoe."

"A shoe?"

Adele said, "Lieutenant, I promise I'll explain everything you want to know in a minute, but do you think you could just tell me what's happened since I called?"

Malmberg considered for a moment.

"Please!"

"All right, all right."

After getting off the phone with Adele at headquarters, Malmberg had sent patrolmen to the front and back of the Bradberry property with instructions not to let anybody leave it.

When Malmberg arrived he had taken three men into the house, and they found the three bodies beneath the heap of sex dolls.

"The woman will be Donna East," Adele said. "The children will be her twins, Cindy and Sally."

Malmberg wrote it down.

"Please, go on."

By the time the police had entered the house, Byron Anthony Bradberry had left the back of the house on foot. He had been easily captured but had denied running to avoid arrest. He had been frightened, he said. There had already been one bogus police officer in his house earlier in the evening and he was afraid when he heard all the noise.

"He has a gun," Adele said. "Did you find it?"

"We found three rifles and several hundred rounds. But the only pistol was a replica. Is that what you mean?"

Adele said nothing. Then she asked, "How were they killed?"

"I don't have the report yet, but it looked like strangulation to me," Malmberg said. Then, "Will you be able to identify them for us?"

"No," Adele said.

"Oh."

"I never met Donna. Any of them."

Malmberg looked unhappy.

"But I know people who can identify her." Thinking of King Smith, of Karen the Cat Lady. "Please go on."

"We showed this Bradberry the bodies in the room. He acted surprised and said that he didn't know anything about it. He *claimed* that he'd let a friend of his use the room, that this guy stayed in the house sometimes as a guest."

"Name?"

Malmberg looked at his notes. "Clint Honneker. He said Honneker'd been at the house earlier in the evening but that he'd left in a hurry and hadn't said why. Just ran out of the house and drove away. But Bradberry also said that Honneker hadn't come in a car, but that his—Bradberry's—car had been stolen earlier in the night." Malmberg shook his head. "It doesn't make a lot of sense."

Adele waited for him to continue.

"Bradberry said he doesn't know where this Honneker is. He says he never asked Honneker about his private life, although he says he knew sometimes he had women in his room. He claims he never realized that Honneker dealt in sex dolls and that he never went into his friend's room. He said we could check it for fingerprints if we liked."

"He's a liar, of course," Adele said.

"We've got Bradberry—and his parents—downtown," Malmberg said. "We only went through the house superficially—they'll do a thorough job in the morning—and all we found that looked like it might mean something was a stack of business cards for this Honneker. A couple of thousand of them."

"Oh. Where did you find them?"

"Not the room we found the bodies in. I think it was Bradberry's own room." Then, "I think it's about time you started telling me what you know, Ms. Buffington, don't you?"

"Can you tell me one more thing?"

"What would that be?"

"One of your detectives, Homer Proffitt, was chasing a car a little before midnight."

"You know something about that, too?" Malmberg asked.

"The car was the one that left the Bradberry house."

"No kidding. I haven't been back to the office. All I know is what came over the radio."

"What happened?"

Adele suddenly felt a dread about what she had asked to hear.

"It was quite a chase," Malmberg said. "But Proffitt finally got the guy off the road at the edge of U.S. 31, near Ekin. Do you know where that is?"

"Is he all right?" Adele asked urgently.

"He's dead," Malmberg said.

"Oh." Adele felt limp.

"Hang on," Malmberg said. "Who do you mean?"

"Proffitt."

"Oh, Proffitt's going to be all right. I thought you were asking about the guy he was chasing."

"*He*'s dead?"

"Yeah. When Proffitt finally got him off the road, the guy came out of the car shooting. Proffitt had to pop him a couple, and he took one in the shoulder himself in the process. But it's not like he's in danger or anything."

"Oh."

"Now," Malmberg said, "do you think I could have the basic facts of what you know? We'll probably be able to wait till tomorrow for a more detailed interview, so all I need is the bare bones."

"Of course," Adele said.

She began to cry.

Bones reminded her of death and Donna East's back-porch garden and the two dead children.

"Jesus," Malmberg complained to Al, "you try to be as gentle and cooperative as you're supposed to be with them these days and what happens but they fall to bits anyway. Jesus!"

Al stuck a finger under Malmberg's nose. "Look, ass-hole, just open your notebook and pick up your pen, and when she feels like talking you listen good."

36

THE doorbell rang at five to ten.

Al left his Wheaties and hurried to answer it. He wanted to keep the bell from ringing a second time.

Outside there was a man of about thirty with black hair.

The man studied Al carefully, his eyes bright, although beneath them were large dark semicircles. The man had one arm in a sling.

Instead of speaking the man smiled as if he'd just heard something funny.

Al said, "Yes?"

The man said, "You wouldn't be the private eye, by any chance?"

Al led Proffitt to the kitchen. He offered coffee.

"Thanks," Proffitt said. He sat down.

Speaking almost in a whisper Al said, "You look awful."

"Shucks, and here I thought I was carrying it off real well."

"Shouldn't you be in the hospital?"

"I was."

"They let you out like that?"

"I expect they know I'm gone by now."

"I see," Al said. "Doing the tough guy routine?"

"There are things that won't wait, Mr. Samson," Proffitt said.

"Just your typical dedicated job-comes-before-everything-else cop, I guess," Al said.

"You know what the job is like," Proffitt said.

"Do I?"

"Don't you? Most of the private detectives I've known were on the force themselves at one point."

"Not me."

"Oh."

"I was in security for a little while," Al said. Which reminded him—for the first time in years—of why he had quit. He'd had to shoot a man. He hadn't liked it. "It was a long, long time ago," Al said.

Proffitt recognized the reflective moment. He sipped from his coffee. "How is Ms. Buffington?"

"Rough."

"I'm sorry."

"I should think you are," Al said. "What the hell can be in your mind to take a civilian into something like that?"

Proffitt looked at him and said, "I am sympathetic about whatever happened, but not regretful."

"Great," Al said.

"I believe very strongly in a person's own responsibility for the consequences of his or her choice of actions. Criminals choose to gamble against society, and I am more than happy to be the instrument that delivers the consequences of that choice to as many of them as I can."

"Are Saturday-morning philosophy lectures meant to be part of your charm?"

"All I'm saying is that last night Adele *decided* to come

with me. I'm sorry it led to trouble for her, but I'm not going to cry salt tears about it."

"One of those guys who sees the world in black and white, huh?"

Proffitt shrugged. "I don't think that's fair."

"Well," Al said, "as far as I'm concerned, it was a stupid, irresponsible thing for *you* to do."

"I don't expect but what there will be plenty of people at headquarters who agree with that assessment."

"I'll damn well see there is."

"You have friends down there?"

"One or two."

"Friends you went off stealing cars with when you were young?"

Al raised an eyebrow. Wondering how close this man and Adele had become. "Shouldn't you caution me before you start an interrogation, Detective?"

Proffitt smiled and drank again. He said, "At least it looks like we found Donna East."

"Adele found Donna East. And the two children."

"We: the police, society."

"Have you—police, society—got it all sorted out? How they were killed, who did it, why?"

"No. I don't know any of that yet," Proffitt said.

"And are you here in an official capacity? To take Adele downtown for a more detailed interview?"

"No, no. I just wanted to know how she was."

"How civilized of you," Al said. And then he felt he was being too unfriendly to the man, that Adele would want him to be more sympathetic.

"I haven't seen anybody at the department today," Proffitt was saying. "I woke up, took a couple of deep breaths, found my clothes and came here."

Al paused. He smiled. "I bet that hurt."

"You win."

"I've been damaged once or twice myself."

"So you know."

"Do you want some breakfast?"

Proffitt considered. "Thank you."

"My morning fix these days is Wheaties and a banana."

"Sounds champion," Proffitt said.

Al put the wherewithal on the table. Proffitt made himself breakfast.

For a few moments they ate.

In silence.

Then there was a noise, and they both looked up to see Adele standing behind Al in the kitchen doorway. She wore a long, white terrycloth bathrobe. She said, "My, my, isn't this sweet!"

Al rose, chewing.

"Ma'am," Proffitt said. He, too, stood, but it was evident that the movement was painful.

"What are you doing up?" Al asked.

"I can go back to sleep after doorbells. But hearing people whisper, whisper, whisper is infuriating."

"Are you hungry?" Al asked.

"Sure."

"Sit down. Eggs and toast and stuff?"

"That would be nice."

Al moved to make food for her, and Adele sat across the table from Proffitt.

She said, "They told me you'd been shot. Are you all right?"

"On the mend, ma'am."

"You look awful!"

"So Mr. Samson tells me. But I expect that only means that feeling better is just around the corner."

"Be careful," Al said. "Prick him and he leaks philosophy."

"Honestly, Homer, you look as if you ought to be lying down somewhere."

"I had some things I wanted to tell you."

"About last night?"

"Well, yes and no."

Adele waited.

"About George Nation."

"Who's that?" Al asked.

"The boyfriend of a woman named Sabrina Caldenwell," Adele said.

"We thought he might have been Ms. Buffington's burglar," Proffitt said.

Adele said, quietly, "It seems a hundred years ago."

"Tuesday night," Proffitt said.

"Yes."

"You remember I had guys keeping an eye on your office?"

"Yes."

"Well, the sucker went back last night."

Adele swallowed. "To the agency?"

"It was after one. My guys saw him go in—that same side window—but because there were only the two of them, they had to wait to take him till he came out."

"And . . . Was it . . . ?"

"George Nation. When they got him down to the lockup they found Brian Wampler's address in his pocket."

"Jesus!" Adele said.

"After they finished the formalities they came to tell me. I was a popular fella last night. There was a line of people come visit me in the hospital. Malmberg stopped by, too, after he left you."

"But that was four A.M."

"He didn't get to me till after five. I think he went back to headquarters first. But I wanted to talk to him, to find out what had happened to you."

"I'm all right," Adele said. "Now."

"Nation isn't saying anything. Except he wants a lawyer. He's been on this ride before."

"I see."

"They'll need you to come in and identify him," Proffitt said.

"Oh," Adele said. Then, "Yes, of course."

"It won't be for a while. Maybe not till tomorrow. He's such a big guy, it will take them some time to get together a lineup with enough other big guys that an identification would stand up in court."

"OK."

"It was a busy night," Proffitt said.

Adele shook her head slowly, images from the Bradberrys' house, from her flight, coming back to her. She took a breath and said, "Tell me what happened at the house."

"I don't really know much, ma'am. I was hoping you would tell me."

"They . . . they found Donna East," Adele said.

"Malmberg said they found some bodies. Has there been positive ID?"

"I have no idea."

"They've probably got that guy Smith down there now."

"I guess."

Proffitt shrugged. "There's a lot we don't know," he said. "But most of it will get sorted out today, with any luck." He paused. "They've given the case to a lieutenant called Turk. Quite a hotshot."

Adele looked at him.

"I wouldn't be allowed," he said. He nodded at his shoulder. "On sick leave."

"What happened to you?" Adele asked.

"I'm . . . I'm sorry to have left you like that."

"I'm a big girl," Adele said.

"Even so."

Al didn't turn from the stove.

Proffitt said, "I heard this car outside and I figured it was the so-called stolen car."

"That's what I thought you thought," Adele said.

"So I went for it."

"So I noticed."

"The driver tried to get out the front, but my car was blocking his way out, so he had to turn around to go for the alley. That's what gave me the time to pick him up. And we had us quite a little ride."

"Lieutenant Malmberg said it was a high-speed chase."

"I think that's a fair enough description," Proffitt said.

"And?"

"Well, there's not much more, except that when I finally got him off the road he turned out to have a weapon, and in the exchange of fire I killed him."

"Oh, dear," Adele said.

"It happens, ma'am."

"Do you know who he was?"

"Malmberg tells me that somebody at the house gave his name as Clint Honneker."

"Yes. The Bradberry's son."

"But when Malmberg talked to me, he had just heard about ID that was on the body."

"Which was?"

"In the name of a Samuel Williams."

Adele's jaw dropped.

"The name means something to you, ma'am?"

The telephone rang.

37

THE caller was Brian Wampler. He was furious and impatient.

He was at the Hendricks Agency. Where Adele had told him, in emphatic terms, to be at ten o'clock, without fail. If she recalled.

She recalled.

He said he'd been a few minutes early and had to wait outside for several minutes. At ten he'd gotten in only because Willy Hendricks had showed up. There had been a break-in overnight and Hendricks was looking at the damage. Hendricks would have called her himself except she was expected at ten. And everyone knew Adele was never late. Did Adele know about the break-in?

She did.

"That's twice in a week," Wampler said.

"I know," she said.

"What is it, open house? No, don't answer that," he said.

"I won't."

"Then I'm waiting around and somebody else comes in. But is it you? No, it's Tina."

"Seeing you must have been a shock for her," Adele said.

"Where the hell are you, Adele?" Brian asked. He was angry. "I'm a busy man. It's absurd enough that you think you can give me orders about where I *have* to be and when, but then to have the fucking nerve not to show up yourself!"

"I am on my way now, Brian."

"Terrific!"

"A lot of strange things happened last night."

"I'm not really very interested in your sex life, dear."

"Whatever you do," Adele said, with all the forceful-ness she could muster, "stay in the office. I guarantee you will regret it if you leave."

It didn't allow much time to think things out. They settled for Adele's cassette recorder supplemented by the latest in high-tech audio-reception organs—the ear.

Al drove Adele. Proffitt followed in his own car.

Adele entered the office alone.

She found Brian Wampler fidgeting near the switch-board. Willy Hendricks was pacing up and down along the wall that housed the agency files. Tina McLarnon was at her desk, hunched over some paperwork.

Wampler spoke first. "I have things to do," he said. "I do not appreciate your threatening me to get here and then fucking me around by being nearly an hour late yourself. I don't care how 'busy' you are, Adele. You either fulfill the responsibilities you take on or you take on fewer responsibilities."

Surprised at her own calmness and control, Adele asked him to go into her office. "Close the door and wait for me. I'll be with you in just a second."

The quiet of her speech in the face of his own evident anger surprised Wampler, too.

He said, "That's just about the amount of time I'm

going to stay." But he went. And he closed the door.

Willy Hendricks had watched the performance. As Wampler went into Adele's office Willy came close and asked in an urgent whisper, "Hey, babe, what the heck is happening? What's that guy doing here and what's all the aggro? I think I got a right to be told, don't you?"

"Willy," Adele said, "I cannot explain one single thing to you now. The police are about to come in and you *must* leave. You want to wait somewhere outside, I'll tell you all about it just as soon as I can."

She went to the door. She beckoned to him and held the door open.

Hendricks couldn't think of any way to go but out.

As he passed her he said, "I'm going to wait. No way should things be going on here that I don't know about."

Adele followed him far enough outside to signal to Proffitt and Al that they should come in.

Hendricks stood and watched the two men enter the agency without speaking.

Adele said, "Not a word, Willy."

She returned to the office and went to Tina, who had been watching the comings and goings.

Al and Proffitt stood either side of Adele's office door and waited.

Tina rose from her desk as Adele approached, but Adele put a finger to her own lips before getting close enough to say in a very low voice, "Please don't ask any questions now, Tina. Just leave your things where they are and go home."

"The most amazing thing has happened with the Clyde case. You remember, the twelve-year-old kid whose grandmother came in?"

"I don't have any time at all. I'll call you at home."

Tina left.

When Adele entered her office, she left the door open. Wampler stood by the window. "Another break-in. What an exciting place this has become." It was not a sympathetic comment.

"Sit down, please," Adele said.

After a moment's resistance, because of the peremptory tone in her voice, Wampler moved from the window and sat.

Adele went to the chair behind her desk. "I asked Tina and Willy to leave," she said. "And they have."

"What the *hell* is all the cloak and dagger?"

"Originally, my insistence on seeing you this morning was because I'd found out that you are still visiting Nora Harrington."

"Nora? What about her?"

"She is not your client anymore, yet you continue to see her without the permission or even the knowledge of her new social worker. That kind of thing is not done, so I wanted to know why you were doing it."

"I feel sorry for her."

"You would no more visit an ex-client because you felt sorry for her than you would cut off your own balls."

"Language, Adele! I'm shocked."

"But I think I've worked out why you visit her for myself."

"Have you indeed?"

"Your new job doesn't take you out at night. But your compulsive need to see other women means it's handy to have an excuse to give Denise when you're out catting. I think visiting Nora occasionally in the evening established that excuse."

Wampler said nothing.

"I'm right, aren't I?"

He shrugged.

"But breach of professional etiquette though that may be, there's a more important reason for me to talk to you this morning."

"And just what would that be?"

"That," Adele said, "would be Donna East."

The name shook Wampler like an electric jolt.

Then he didn't move, even to breathe. His eyes were wide open, but not as wide as his mouth.

Adele watched him, her own anger, fury and hatred almost spilling out, giving her a need to rush at him, to hit him, to hurt him.

Although her muscles tensed, she stayed where she was.

She said, "Your new job is at the Hoosier Placement Center. A private adoption agency. Your boss there is Samuel Williams."

He didn't move.

Slowly, clearly, she said, "Samuel Williams was Donna East's welfare worker. He set up the Hoosier Placement Center and only stayed at Welfare till it became big enough for him to quit."

Adele paused again. Then she said, "Samuel Williams was killed in a shoot-out with the police last night."

This finally jerked Wampler back to some form of life.

He coughed and breathed and twitched.

He said, "I only ever dealt with the adopters."

"What?"

"I swear, Adele, I swear on my mother's grave, I never knew where he got the babies from."

38

BRIAN Wampler began to cry.

Adele felt disgust and no compassion.

She waited.

Wampler sniffled to a stop. He began to talk.

"Sam Williams called me about five months ago. When the Sabrina Caldenwell thing was blowing up."

"Did you know him before?"

"No. Well, not really, I think I'd met him. I knew the name, the way we've all kind of heard the names of other social workers, if they've been in the game for any length of time."

"Go on."

"Sam said that he had started this private adoption agency on the side. He'd set it up, with a partner, while he was still with Welfare. The partner had some financing and they ran it under the partner's name, because if Welfare had known how involved he was they wouldn't have approved."

"Too right," Adele said.

"But the agency grew fast, so Sam quit Welfare. And he said it was the smartest move he ever made."

"And?"

"He said he'd heard from various sources that I have this way with people, this kind of personableness." Wampler shrugged. "Can I help how I am?"

Adele kept herself from saying anything.

"Sam said he needed someone like me to deal with prospective adoptive parents. He was sounding me out about the job. It was mostly in the office and it was regular hours. The money was decent to start and it could get a lot better. Might I be interested?"

"And you were."

"Given that there *was* a lot of trouble about Sabrina—not that I ever did anything wrong there—well, sure, in the circumstances how could I not be interested? So I met him, and he went through exactly what he wanted and he offered it to me, and I damn well jumped at it."

"And you've been there, what, four months?"

Wampler nodded. He looked intensely into Adele's eyes. "Honest to God, I thought it was a straight operation. I really did."

"And of course it isn't," Adele said, as if she already knew everything there was to know.

"What he's been doing is *grotesque*," Wampler said. He put his hands up to his face again. From behind his hands Wampler said, "I knew pretty early on that we had too many babies." He snuffled. He began to cry again.

Adele said, "Cut the bullshit tears, Brian. I don't believe them for a minute."

Wampler shook his head bitterly. He dropped his hands. He said, "I have feelings. You may never have gone for me and you many think I'm shallow shit, but I *have* feelings. If I didn't have feelings I would never have gotten into this business in the first place." He stared at Adele to prove his point.

Adele stared back.

"God, you're a hard bitch!" he said. He wiped his eyes

with his arm. He said, "There just aren't *that* many healthy babies these days that the girls want to give away. They keep most of them. You know that. You see it all the time."

"So did you ask Williams about the babies?"

"I commented on it." Wampler scratched at an ear. He rubbed his nose. "I was the new boy in the setup. I could hardly push it."

"And he said . . . ?"

"That he had a special rapport with unwed mothers. Some social workers were cold and went by the book. Others, like us—him and me—we had a way with people and we could make them understand things, like about the importance of thinking of their babies' futures."

"And you bought that, did you?"

"For a while. He was my boss. I was only in the job a few weeks."

"So what happened?"

"One day last month I found some records." He rocked his head slowly from side to side. "It was a quiet day. It was cold. Nobody else was around. I was bored. We even used to get days like that here."

Adele said nothing.

"I thought the more I knew about the agency the better I could do my job. I started going through some files."

"And?"

"I found that a lot of the babies we were placing came from mothers who had placed babies through us before."

"And you asked him about that?"

Wampler closed his eyes and exhaled heavily. With his eyes still closed he said, "Sam *farmed* those girls, Adele. He farmed them for babies."

There was a moment during which they were both deathly still.

Wampler said, "Sam or his partner—both of them I think. They went around."

"I know about the so-called polling."

"Well, they would go into poor areas and they would find these girls who lived alone. Or women. Maybe teenagers who had come to Indianapolis from someplace else and didn't know many people. Women who maybe had been abandoned here and didn't have ties."

"People like Donna East."

"Yeah." He shrugged. "Sam knew that one from when he worked Welfare, but she was the type. They were looking for girls who were passive, the kind without much initiative, the kind they could influence, and take over. Girls who would respond to attention."

"I see," Adele said, as she began to.

"And when they found one, what they would do was move her from where she was living to someplace completely new, where she didn't know anybody. Then they'd keep her as isolated as they could. She'd be completely dependent for food and clothes and a place to live. And then they would keep her pregnant and they would take the babies when they came."

"And place them for adoption through the agency."

"Sell them, Adele. They'd sell them."

"Oh." Then, "Jesus."

"Sometimes maybe the girl would already have older kids. They'd place those, too, if they could. If they were healthy. But it was the newborn babies that were at a premium. They were selling babies all over the country. Even some from outside the country. And a few time times the prospective father came in to make the girl pregnant himself. Once a guy made three girls pregnant on condition that he would take all the boys. It was growing like crazy. They were talking about fertility drugs to get twins and triplets. They already have a doctor lined up. And the money that is involved sometimes . . . You wouldn't believe."

"And Williams just *told* you about this?"

"Yes," Wampler said. "The day I went through the

files. He came back and saw what I was doing and he talked about it." Head down. "He was proud of it."

"And wasn't he worried that you would tell the police?"

"He *said* he wasn't afraid of the police. He *said* they might be working near the edge of the law but that the way they kept the records it would be very very tough to get them convicted of anything. He laughed about it."

"And?"

"Then he said he'd always intended to make me a more active part of the operation eventually and maybe it was just as well that it was sooner rather than later. He said that because I had been in social work for a long time I even ought to know a few likely candidates. He had four ex-clients of his own in the 'system.' That was one of the reasons he'd come to me, that I worked for an agency with a lot of child abuse."

Adele waited.

Wampler said, "But the main reason he'd come to me was that he'd heard I was about to have my butt kicked to hell and back about Sabrina Caldenwell. Lose my job for sure and maybe worse. He'd figured that I'd do just about anything to get out of the situation and that I wouldn't be in a position to do too much moralizing."

He paused. He was breathing hard.

"And he was just about right," Adele said, more gently.

"Yeah."

She waited for him.

Wampler shrugged. "Then Sam started talking that there wasn't much of a moral issue involved anyway. He said that I had been in social work long enough to know damn well that there was a class of people who would spend their lives just having babies anyway, that they weren't good for anything else and that really what we were doing was helping the children. They'd have a chance to have better lives. And we were helping the adoptive parents. And helping the mothers too, even if they didn't necessarily know it."

"And helping yourselves," Adele said.

"Honest to God, Adele, I didn't have a clue about any of this until a few weeks ago. And I just didn't know what to do."

"You've know about it for *weeks* and you *sat* on it?"

"Put yourself in my position!"

Adele did not respond to this suggestion. Instead she said, "What about Donna East?"

Wampler's eyes dropped.

"I didn't have anything to do with that."

"But you knew about it."

"I knew that there was a problem."

"What was the problem?"

"She wasn't pregnant."

Adele stared.

"She'd gone several months since her last baby and she wasn't pregnant. Sam's partner—"

"Bradberry?"

"Yes. Because Sam had known her from before, she was one of the ones Bradberry dealt with. Bradberry had this talk with her. He finally found out that when she was in the hospital having the last kid, some doctor had offered to sterilize her and she had let him do it."

"The poor woman," Adele said quietly.

"We'd only had two babies off her. And our doctor wasn't all that sure he could reverse the sterilization. So," Wampler said, "she was a problem."

"And did you know how they were going to solve the problem?" Adele was unable to ask the question without her voice becoming harsh.

"Sam said Bradberry had a plan. Actually, the idea was from some old Indiana law."

"Brian . . ."

"Back in the days before statehood—"

"What are you talking about now?" Angrily.

"I'm only telling you what Sam said to me."

"Yes. Well." Adele thought of the listening ears outside her door.

"Back then—we're talking early 1800's—when they had a family go bankrupt, what they did was hold an auction."

Adele looked at Wampler.

"They asked people in the community to make bids. They bid what was the least amount of money from the government they would take to bring the bankrupt people into their houses and feed them. Whoever made the lowest bid got the bankrupt family. Or they'd split families. Whatever it took."

"That happened in Indiana?"

"Yeah. It was an idea that started in New Hampshire."

"And . . . ?"

"Well, what Sam said was that this Bradberry guy was going to auction Donna East off. Contact some people he knew, see what they would give him for her—you know, either as a kind of long-term unpaid servant. Or as . . . Well, that's what the idea was."

"And what did Bradberry plan to do with the two girls?"

"They'd already been . . . adopted. Long time ago."

"I mean the two who lived with her."

"I only know about the two babies she had. Last year and the year before."

"There were two girls who lived with her who had Down's syndrome, and another, older daughter."

"I don't know anything about those children, Adele. Honestly. And I don't know any of the details about where she went, or who she's with."

"Brian . . ."

"What?"

"Donna East's body was found in Bradberry's house last night."

"Her . . . body?"

"And the two girls who lived with her. They were murdered, Brian."

"Murdered?"

He didn't cry this time. He wailed.

39

PROFFITT arrested Brian Wampler and read him his rights. Wampler was hysterical and begging to give information against Williams and Bradberry. It didn't matter that Williams was already dead.

Wampler was handcuffed and loaded into the back of Proffitt's car. Proffitt drove him downtown.

In Al's van Al and Adele followed. They didn't talk much.

Initially at police headquarters it was a question of who would get Adele first: Diehl working on the Other Wampler killing or Turk working on the Donna East case.

When Adele realized this she said to Al, "All I feel like doing is going home and sleeping."

In fact, Diehl still wasn't ready yet with his lineup.

And Turk wanted to hear what Proffitt had to say, before she interviewed either Adele or Brian Wampler.

So Wampler was taken to the fifth floor to wait in the police lockup.

Al insisted that he be allowed to take Adele home. There was no need for her to wait at headquarters. It wasn't an emergency. Everyone involved was in custody. It was just a matter of sorting out exactly what had happened. She would be at home when they wanted her.

No one actually said, "Go on home, then," but when he led Adele out, no one moved to stop them.

Adele slept.
Al stayed at the house all day.
Lucy came home in the middle of the afternoon.

Al hadn't known she was out. Everyone had left the house in the morning before Lucy, or Fritz, had surfaced.

Al met Lucy in the hallway. She was intending to talk to her mother, to see if she *really* didn't mind her having men in overnight, because if she didn't that might solve a lot of things.

Al wouldn't let Lucy wake her mother up. Instead he sat her down and explained the kinds of thing that Adele had been through.

Lucy said, "And I thought I had problems."

Adele appeared about six.

The police had still not called or come. Al was a little surprised about that, but he was pleased.

When Adele came into the living room, the first thing she did was to ask about Billie, Donna East's oldest child. The girl had been "lost" somewhere between Donna's life in Karen the Cat Lady's building and her life in King Smith's building. "Brian said that all they'd had from Donna was two babies. Didn't he?"

"Yes."

"And there were only the two girls killed with her."

Only.

"Yes."

"Make sure I remember to ask Homer about Billie," Adele said.

"I will."

"Al, I'm terribly hungry."

Al considered her hunger a good sign.

He sent Lucy out for pizza and beer.

While Lucy was out, Homer Proffitt arrived.

When Al answered the door, Proffitt looked old and exhausted and about to die.

In better light he looked even worse.

Adele was subtle. She asked, "Does your arm hurt a lot?"

Proffitt blinked. "What? Oh, my arm. I'd forgotten about it."

Adele made room on the couch. Proffitt sat.

"Homer, is something wrong?" she asked.

"Yes."

She waited.

Al waited.

Proffitt did not speak.

Al asked, "Would you like a drink?"

Proffitt did not respond.

Al and Adele looked at each other. Then Adele took one of Proffitt's hands and asked, "What's happened?"

"Somehow . . ." Proffitt began. And then stopped.

"What?"

"Somehow when they put Brian Wampler in the lockup, they put him in the same cage they were holding George Nation in."

Adele stared.

"Nation broke Wampler's neck and back and jaw and skull and both his legs."

"Is . . . ?"

"Wampler was dead in the first couple of minutes. They say Nation worked on him for nearly ten before anyone was able to pull him off the body."

40

PROFFITT ate a little pizza. He took a sip from a can of beer.

Then he threw up.

Al helped him to the guest bedroom, and moments after he was tucked in Proffitt was asleep.

Back in the dining room Adele and Al ate in nibbles. Lucy tried to make small talk, but struggled to find a line between her mother's troubles and her own burgeoning romance. She felt she shouldn't talk about the one, and she could hardly bear not to talk about the other.

Adele helped after a bit. She said, "Fritz seems a nice boy."

"Yes," Al said.

Lucy beamed and bubbled agreement and had large samples of Adele's and Al's pizzas.

Then the telephone rang. Lucy nearly choked in her rush to answer it.

The caller was Fritz.

When Lucy came back she asked, "Is it all right if I go out?"

"Of course," her mother said. Then said, "Come here a minute."

The two women shared a long hug.

When Lucy left the room to get ready, her face was flushed. She spent half an hour picking what to wear. Adele said, "I can't remember when the last time she asked permission to go out was."

Adele and Al turned the television on, and Al answered the telephone when it rang.

The call was from Tina McLarnon. She said she understood that Adele had had a hard day but that she, Tina, was going out. She asked Al to take a long message and give it to Adele when Adele was up to it.

Al took it.

The message was that Clyde the grandson had not been copulating with the neighbor girls after all. That what the grandmother had seen was the children kissing.

"Kissing?" Adele asked.

"Tina says that kissing is what the grandmother thought makes babies."

"Hang on," Adele said, "hang on—"

"Tina will tell you all about it when you're back at the office, but the basics are that Granny only ever did 'it' once. She was drunk at the time and all she remembers was kissing the guy. She raised her daughter single-handed. She thinks kissing is sexual intercourse."

"I don't believe this," Adele says.

"I don't know your Tina," Al said. "Is she the kind who would make up a story like that?"

"No."

Al shook his head. He said, "Think of all the images of kissing there are in the world. People on the street, on TV, in movies, in magazines. Suppose each time, instead of kissing, they *were* actually at *it*. What kind of world must this woman have been living in?"

Adele said, "I wonder if Tina is going out with her musician."

* * *

Proffitt appeared in the kitchen at nine-thirty in the morning. He looked better.

Al and Adele were nursing coffees and sharing sections of the *Star*.

"Great story in the paper this morning," Al said. "A guy in Hobart died from being hit on the head thirty-five times with a hammer, and the local police have decided that he committed suicide."

Proffitt smiled faintly and sat down at the table.

Adele said, "Al went out for some Wheaties."

Proffitt nodded in acknowledgment.

Adele said, "Do you want some, Homer?"

He said, "There is something I need to do today. It has to be done now. If we stay here, we'll get caught up in all the red tape downtown." He raised the arm in the sling. "I hate to ask, ma'am, but will you drive me?"

After talking it through, Adele decided that she preferred Al to stay home to answer the phone and explain where they had gone and when they would be back. She just about felt up to the driving.

41

PROFFITT spotted the mailbox on State 62 that had EAST painted on the side. They turned onto the track that led off the road. The sun was high in the west. The day was cold.

The farmhouse was a cream-colored wooden building in need of a lick of paint. Behind it a rust-brown barn and two smaller buildings looked better taken care of. An old Ford pickup rested beside the house.

As Proffitt and Adele pulled to a stop, a child opened the front door and stood inside the glass of the storm door, watching.

The child's hair was short and yellow. He or she had the wide-eyed curiosity of a youngster not accustomed to strangers.

Proffitt and Adele got out and approached the porch.

The child departed suddenly as they got to the bottom of the steps, leaving the door open.

Proffitt and Adele climbed to the porch. They stood and waited, knowing that adults had been summoned more surely than by any doorbell.

Sure enough a tall, lean woman with short gray hair came to the door. She was in her mid-fifties and wore a long light-blue dress and a red apron. She opened the storm door and said, "Yes?"

Proffitt said, "Mrs. East?"

"That's me."

The child peeked out from behind the woman's skirt.

"My name is Homer Proffitt, ma'am. I came out here once while I was with the Evansville Police, on a matter having to do with some bones that were found on your land that they thought might be human remains."

"I think I recall you," the woman said.

"Well, ma'am, I work with the Indianapolis Police now and I've come down to have a little word with you and your husband."

"Them bones wasn't recent bones," the woman said. "They got that all sorted out."

"I know, ma'am. I'm the one did the sorting. This here is about something different."

"All right. You better come in."

The woman opened the door for Proffitt and Adele. She said to the child, "Billie, you go get your grandpa."

The child looked at Proffitt, then back at her grandmother. She took a breath and pushed past the visitors and ran toward the outbuildings.

Proffitt and Adele followed Mrs. East to her front room.

When they were settled, Proffitt asked Mrs. East, "Is the child your daughter Donna's little girl, ma'am?"

The woman eyed first Proffitt, then Adele. "You come to tell me Donna's dead, ain't you?"

"It's just when your husband comes, ma'am, I think it might be as well if the little girl went to play somewheres else."

The sound of footsteps on the porch preceded the entry of the child. Then Billie burst in and said, "Grandpa's wiping his feet."

"OK, honey," Mrs. East said. "Now these folks have

come on business, Billie. You go feed the chickens."

"But it ain't time."

"It's nearly time. And I don't know when we're going to be finished."

Billie said, "Don't want to."

"Go on now, hear?"

Sulkily, Billie left for the back of the house as a thick-chested man with wrinkled skin but startlingly yellow hair entered the room through the front door.

"How do," the man said. "Calvin East." He offered Proffitt a hand, which Proffitt stood and shook. "Ma'am, he said to Adele. Then, to his wife, "What's it all about then, Nellie?"

"They ain't said yet."

Calvin East sat by his wife. "Billie tells me you're a policeman," he said to Proffitt. He squinted. "I know you."

"The bones," Nellie East said.

"Ah, the bones. This is the young feller that sorted it all out."

"That's right," Proffitt said, "but I work for the Indianapolis Police Department now."

"Indianapolis, huh?" East looked at his wife.

"It's about your daughter, Donna, Mr. East," Proffitt said.

"I thought it might be," East said. "With the two boys dead and gone, she's about the only one left it could be about." He took his wife's hand.

Proffitt and Adele sat in a diner on the main road in De Gonia Springs.

Adele felt utterly flat. The Easts' stoicism had disturbed her deeply. Accepting their last child's death was one thing—they had not expected good things after she had run off in the first place. But their description of their last contact with Donna—who had telephoned after years of silence to say she was sending Billie to them on a bus—had moved Adele deeply.

Mrs. East had ended up having to comfort Adele, instead of the other way around. "Things happen, honey," Mrs. East had said. "Things happen. You can't foresee 'em."

"But it isn't right!" Adele had said.

"You can't do no more than your best," Mrs. East had said, "and take what comes."

A waitress came for their orders.

Adele didn't care what she ate, and said so. Proffitt ordered for them both.

When the waitress left, Adele asked, "How *can* the Easts just let things wash over them like that?"

"What would you have them do, ma'am?"

"Cry. Stamp their feet. Hit out. Hit *us!*"

"They'll cry in their own time."

"Yes. All right. But the 'virtue' of their passiveness, their country wisdom . . . All it really amounts to is a way to excuse when bad people do bad things. If it were up to them, they would just sit down and *let* things like that happen."

"And you're not able to take what happens in life that way," Proffitt said.

"No, I'm not. I can't sit back and not try to make things better. And neither can you."

"True enough, I guess." Proffitt said. "But in the end, ma'am, do you figure we're any the better off for it?"

Later, in the car as they headed for Indianapolis, Adele answered his question. "Yes," she said. "I damn well do."